A Fairytale Reality

Helen Claringbull

DEDICATION

For all my truly wonderful family and friends. Thank you for your unending support and encouragement. I would not have been able to embark on this journey without you.

BOOKS BY THE AUTHOR IN SEQUENCE

THE GREATEST GIFT
A FAIRYTALE CHRISTMAS
A FAIRYTALE REALITY

ACKNOWLEDGMENTS

With thanks to my mum, Elizabeth Claringbull, for her editing notes.

Thanks also to all those who read and reviewed my first two novels, and who encouraged me to keep writing. Once again, this novel is for you.

SYNOPSIS

Madeline Lane travelled to America for Christmas, and came home heartbroken, having loved and lost during that wonderful holiday.

Adam Baynes fell in love with a beautiful woman who captured his heart during a brief encounter and made him face up to the reality he'd hidden from for so long.

Jim McDonald has been grieving the loss of his wife in a hit and run accident and is now starting to rebuild his life with the support of his family.

Francesca Marten and Ed Smithers found that a chance encounter on New Year's Eve, together with some rather surprising family news, would change the course of their lives and their family forever.

The lives of these five people become intrinsically joined, as fairytales and reality collide in this, the third novel by author Helen Claringbull.

Lane Family Tree

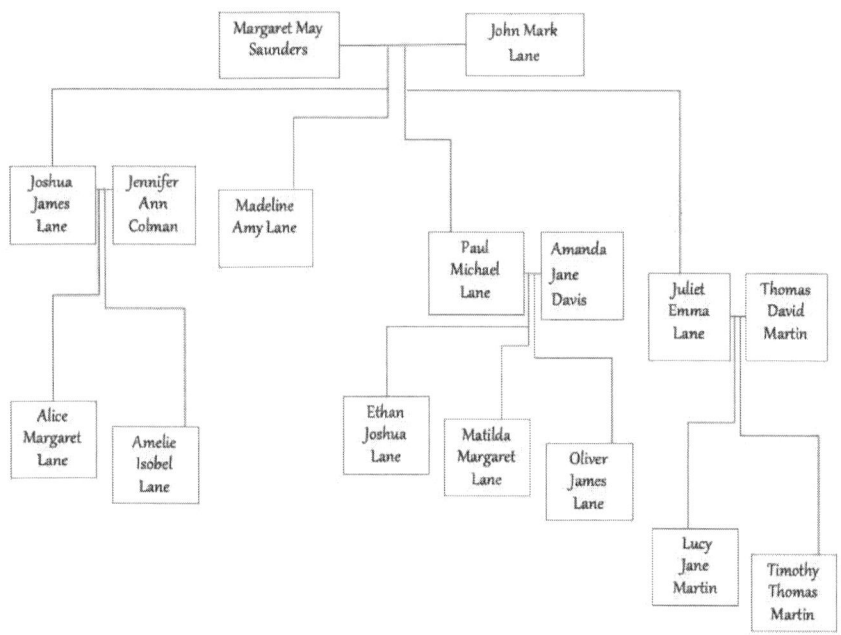

Baynes Family Tree

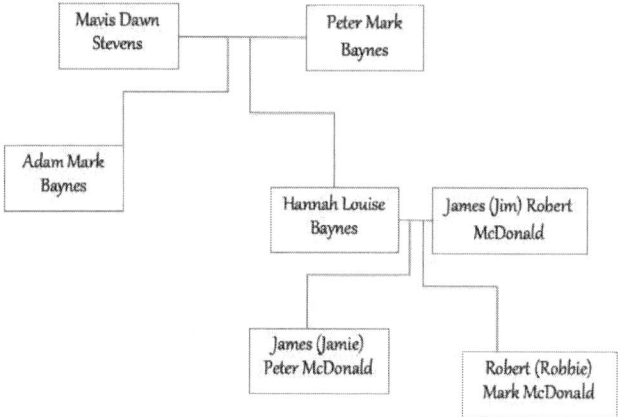

Marten Family Tree

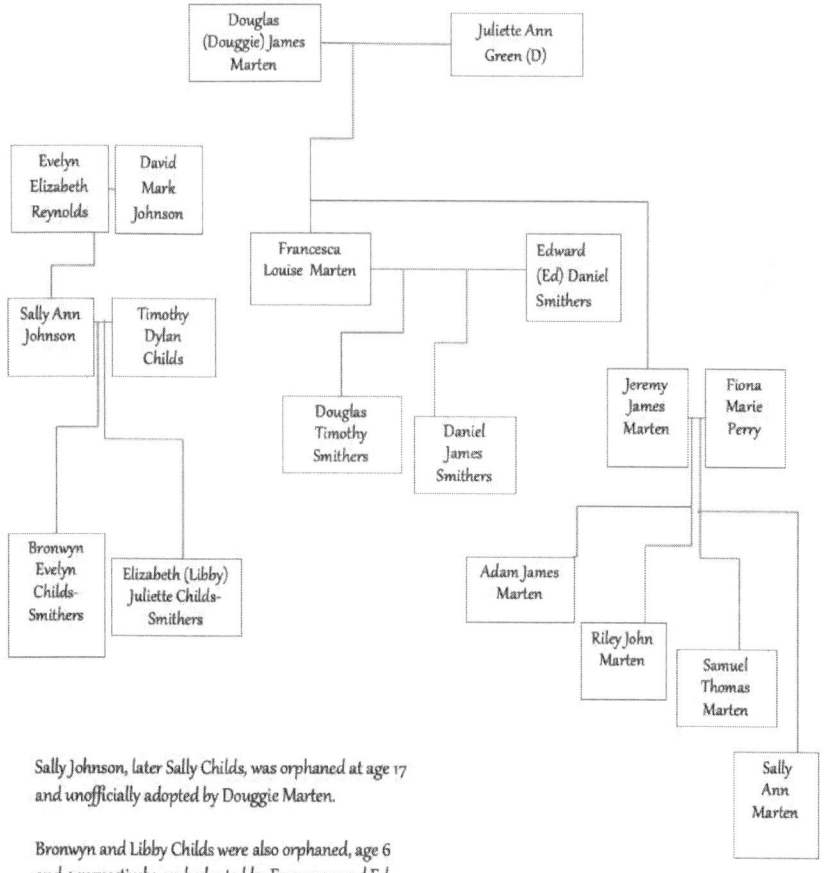

Sally Johnson, later Sally Childs, was orphaned at age 17 and unofficially adopted by Douggie Marten.

Bronwyn and Libby Childs were also orphaned, age 6 and 4 respectively, and adopted by Francesca and Ed Smithers.

1

Maddie twisted herself in Adam's arms and curled her body further into his. She couldn't quite believe her luck. Here she was, snuggled up in bed, full of hope and anticipation for the new year ahead of her, and knowing now that one way or the other, her future lay with this gorgeous man that she'd met in New York just 10 days earlier. A gorgeous man who was, indeed, now sleeping soundly beside her in her bed. Maddie was head over heels in love. The previous night had been very intense, not least their lovemaking. It was as if they had to make up for so much lost time, yet in reality, it had only been a few days since they'd seen each other.

When she'd heard a knock on the door of her modest three bed semi the previous evening, whilst her New Year's Eve gathering for family and friends was in full swing, Maddie had never in a million years expected it to be Adam who walked into her jam packed lounge a few moments later. Maddie's sister Juliet had volunteered to open the door, as there must have been at least twenty people squeezed into the not particularly large lounge when Adam had arrived, and Juliet had been far closer to the hallway, and therefore far more capable of getting to the door to greet the guest, than Maddie had been. As Juliet had ushered a slightly frightened looking Adam into the lounge a few minutes later, Maddie felt like her heart had exploded. Everything seemed to happen in slow motion. She had dreamed of seeing him again, and even tried to contact him earlier that day, despite prior promises to herself that she would try to move on, having ended their fledgling relationship with very good reason before boarding her plane home from New York, but she never for a moment thought that he would actually turn up unannounced in her home. She knew that his mother had her address, having issued an open invitation to Mavis, and Adam's father Peter, telling them that they would be very welcome to visit her at any time, but she didn't imagine for a second that Adam would return to England with them on New Year's Eve, as this had certainly not been his plan when they had parted.

Seeing Adam again had made her insides go all queasy; that butterflies feeling you get when you're either really nervous or totally over excited. At that point Maddie couldn't say whether the feelings she was experiencing were due to nerves, excitement or a mixture of both, but she definitely felt like her insides were doing somersaults as she walked slowly towards him. Feeling the crowded room disperse, yet knowing full well that everyone was looking at her and gauging her reaction, not least her beau, she moved in his direction. As he closed the remaining distance between them and began talking, explaining that he was determined to make a life for them together, despite the obstacles they both knew they had to overcome, Maddie felt an overwhelming sense of calm and relief. Neither of them had any idea of how the logistics of being together would pan out, and indeed Maddie didn't know then of Adam's plan to relocate back to England, but something in her heart told her that their story was far from over and this New Year's Eve would herald new beginnings for both of them. She was certain that 2020 would be the best year of her life.

As they kissed, her friends and family who were gathered around them cheered and whooped warmly. Maddie knew that they wanted nothing more than for her to be happy, and several of them had encouraged her not to give up on the relationship which had been born in New York a few days earlier. They were all excited to meet Adam, and it transpired that one of the other guests, Ed, had worked with Adam in Canary Wharf many years ago, which only served to reassure Maddie that this was meant to be and that Adam really was one of the good guys, because knowing Ed made him more of a known quantity. She didn't know Ed particularly well herself; he was the brother-in-law of her best friend from University, Fiona, but she'd first made his acquaintance ten years ago, and it appeared he'd known Adam for more than double that amount of time.

Finally managing to escape from the well-wishers for a few minutes, Maddie guided Adam out into the conservatory where they sat on the wicker garden furniture that she kept in there. It was chilly, being the middle of winter in a room that she never bothered to heat, but it was quiet and mercifully, the other guests had respected their need for some time alone. Adam told Maddie that he'd been doing a lot of soul searching since she had left him in New York five days earlier, and with the help and support of his parents he had come to recognise that he no longer wanted to hide away on the other side of the world, where he had been metaphorically burying his head in the sand. He now knew that he wanted more from life than smart possessions, a swanky penthouse apartment and a high powered job that was all consuming, and recognised that he needed to make changes. What he really wanted was to face up to his emotions, to overcome his fear of committing to a relationship in case he got hurt again, and to try and build a life back in the UK where he would not only have the love and support of his family and friends, but more importantly, he could plan a future with the girl who had captured his heart.

These words were exactly what Maddie had been desperately hoping to hear, although not really daring to believe possible. There were so many things to discuss, and several hurdles to leap over in order that they could spend the rest of their lives together, but knowing it was what both of them wanted gave them hope. They were both strong, independent people, albeit a little scared and scarred emotionally. They were also both confirmed singletons until a few days before, which meant that adapting to life as part of a pair would bring its own challenges, but they knew that if they worked together to the same end goal, anything was possible.

Adam told Maddie that he had initially planned to resign from his company, whilst still maintaining the stocks and shares he held, as his position as CEO of a New York based firm was not tenable if he was based in London, however he'd then done some further research and investigation into the company's international operation during the journey from the States to England, and believed it might be possible to branch out and run a subsidiary company from the UK. This was obviously going to require the approval of the Board, and would require a lot of time and effort to build a company from the ground up in London, but he felt that as a major shareholder and the current company director, he had a fair chance of convincing his colleagues to let him run with the idea, and he knew that hard work was something he was good at.

Adam's only reservation in all of this was the promise that he had made to himself to spend more time with his family, and to build a life with Maddie, which would potentially be counter intuitive to starting a company from the ground up, but Maddie knew that she needed to encourage him to run with his dreams. "You will have quite a balancing act on your hands" she said, as he discussed his inner conflict, "but I promise you that I won't let you return to being a workaholic, and I know your parents will hold you accountable to them too. If you move back to England and take just any old job that pays the bills, you won't be happy, and then you'll start to resent giving up on your business and that will lead to resentment of me and of your family". Adam shook his head vigorously, but Maddie gently put her finger to his lips, effectively silencing him so that she could continue.

"No, listen to me, hear me out, please" she pleaded. "If you want to do this, and if it gives you a new challenge which you relish, and which excites you, then I will support you every step of the way. I don't want you to turn your life upside down for me, because if I'm the only motivation you have to return to the UK then our relationship is doomed to fail, but if branching out in London is the way forward for your company, and a challenge that you want to take on, then that gives you a purpose in life and it means you're not just coming home for me, you're coming home for the same reason you left in the first place; for work, and us being together is a happy bonus of that".

Deep down, Adam had known she was right. After all, he'd spent the entire flight back to England desperately trying to find ways to segue the work he loved with his other passion; Maddie. This was the best he'd come up with, and initially when the idea had come to him it seemed like a pipedream, but the more he massaged the figures and investigated the logistics, the more potential the idea seemed to have to become a reality. He had begun working on a proposal for the Board of Directors during the flight and was actually quite pleased with the result. If he had Maddie's support too, then that would be a huge incentive to push the idea forward, but he wasn't convinced that his parents would be quite so on board with the idea.

"I don't think Mum and Dad are going to be too keen on me expanding the business and setting up a new branch of the firm" he said, voicing his concerns. "I think they're hoping I'll go back to a nine to five job in the city or better still, something based in the suburbs. A start up business can be all consuming and I doubt they'll be too keen on the idea because they'll worry that I'll be just as distant from them as I was in New York" Adam explained.

"No." said Maddie firmly. "You won't be distant, because neither I nor they will let you be. I really believe that you doing this will be the best chance we have of making our relationship work, because the man I fell in love with had drive and passion and determination and you'd lose that if you were doing a job you weren't fully invested in. I want you to be the man I met in New York, but I want you here too. I want the best of both worlds, and I'm sure the same goes for your parents". Adam didn't know what more to say. He leant over and kissed her passionately, trying to communicate with his actions all the love, respect, admiration and gratitude that he was feeling in that moment.

They were interrupted by Timmy, Maddie's young nephew, bursting into the room.

"Errguhh" he exclaimed as the couple jumped apart. "It's almost midnight Auntie Mads. Mum sent me to come and get you and tell you that you've got to come back in now".

Following the young boy back into the lounge, Maddie and Adam were both handed a glass of prosecco. Swapping hers quickly for a glass of red wine, not being a fan of anything fizzy and having had one too many bad experiences with fizzy wine in the past, they joined everyone in the lounge, watching the New Year's Eve broadcast from London on the television. As the countdown to midnight began, everyone in the room, young and old, joined in.

"Ten, Nine, Eight, Seven, Six, Five, Four, Three, Two, One, Happy New Year!".

Lots of hugging and kissing ensued and then everyone linked hands to sing Auld Lang Syne, accompanied by those singing on the television.

Most of the guests had left shortly after midnight, having young children to get home to bed. Maddie's old university friend Fiona had insisted on staying and helping with the clear up process, and Juliet had jumped on her bandwagon, mainly thought Maddie, so that she could interrogate her sister, which had probably also been Fiona's motive, although helping was more in character for Fiona than for Juliet. They had stood in the kitchen chatting, whilst packing away the leftover food, loading the dishwasher and tidying up, and Jules had immediately pounced on her sister requesting information "So what did he say Mads?".

Fiona was marginally more subtle. "I'm guessing that Adam's arrival is good news?". Maddie had recounted briefly the discussions she and Adam had in the conservatory, explaining to her friends that whilst she knew there were still a lot of details to work through, she thought that she and Adam stood a good chance of building a future together. She then said, not quite as politely as she maybe could have done, that she would very much like it if all her guests were to vacate the premises now, or "bugger off home" as she put it, so that she and Adam could spend some time alone.

Having waved off the last of the partygoers, Maddie gave Adam a brief guided tour of her home, which didn't take long as the property, although three bedroomed, with two reception rooms and a conservatory, was still very small in comparison to Adam's huge apartment in New York. "It's not quite as impressive as yours, but it's mine. Well, it's mine and the mortgage company's really" she corrected herself, "and it's comfortable and most importantly, it's my home."

Adam smiled and took her in his arms. "I think it's absolutely lovely, just like his owner" he crooned, and with that comment, he kissed her passionately once again, and led her into the main bedroom. There was to be no more talking until morning.

2

Maddie woke with a start, having drifted off to sleep again, and realised that she was alone in bed. Had last night really happened? Had she dreamed it? Was it only New Year's Eve and did she still have a party to plan and organise? So many questions rushed through her mind as she roused herself from her dazed and fuzzy state. Feeling a stab of bitter disappointment that she was alone after all, she hauled herself out of bed and pulled on her fluffy dressing gown. It was then that she spotted Adam's watch on the nightstand on his side of the bed and saw that his shoes were still on the floor beside the bed. It hadn't been a dream. Adam really was here, except he wasn't in the room, so where could he be?

Making her way downstairs, and wishing that perhaps she'd not drunk quite so much wine the night before, as her head was feeling just a little bit fuzzy this morning, Maddie made her way into the kitchen to find Adam swearing at the coffee machine.

"Oh come on you stupid thing, all I want you to do is brew some bloody coffee!".

"Good morning to you too" Maddie responded sarcastically, laughing at the gorgeous man standing bare foot in her kitchen who was clearly clueless as to how to work that particular piece of technology. His demeanour changed instantly, as he took her in his arms and kissed the top of her head.

"Good morning gorgeous". He said simply. "I was going to bring you a cup of coffee in bed, but I couldn't get the damn machine to do anything". Maddie adjusted herself slightly in his embrace, reached over and pressed two buttons and, as if by magic, the machine whirred to life and began brewing coffee.

"How the hell did you do that?" he asked, somewhat incredulously, having spent a good fifteen minutes trying to work out how to make the machine work.

"Practice". Maddie replied simply, and lent into his warm body again, relishing the feel of his arms wrapped around her.

Two cups of coffee brewed, the couple made their way into the lounge, which still bore the aftermath of what had clearly been a good party the night before.

"This is going to take some cleaning up" Maddie remarked as they sat down on one of her big comfy sofas, yet making no move to actually start the process.

"It was a great party though" Adam commented.

"Yes, and even better for you showing up" she replied.

As it was, the clear up process was relatively quick and painless, and before long Maddie was making more mess in the kitchen, cooking them both a full English breakfast.

"Do I get this treatment every day from now on?" Adam asked, as he watched her move around the kitchen.

"To be honest, I wouldn't usually bother, and certainly not when I'm alone, but I figured today was a special day. I do sometimes do this for guest though, so you might be lucky, but don't expect it on a work day. It takes too long to prepare and clean up when I have to be out of the house in a hurry!".

Adam laughed. "It's fine. I don't think my waistline could take it all the time either. Special occasions will be nice though". Maddie smiled, and continued cooking. She felt thoroughly content.

Once they'd breakfasted, and Maddie had showered and dressed, the couple set out for Mavis and Peter's house.

"Mum and Dad will be so pleased to see you again" Adam said from the passenger seat, as Maddie reversed her car out of the driveway and onto the main road.

"I'm looking forward to seeing them again too" she said warmly, thinking back to how scared she'd been at the prospect of first meeting them a week ago, and how fond she had become of them, and obviously of their son too, in such a short space of time.

Mavis was indeed absolutely thrilled to see Maddie again, and even happier that Adam seemed to be so content. She was his mother, and she had supported his move to America as she had known it was the right thing for him to do at the time, but it didn't mean that she'd liked it and she certainly wasn't going to try and dissuade him from his plan to return to England permanently. She wanted to have her family as close as possible now, and Adam's initial meeting with Maddie had paved the way for that to happen.

Explaining that she had sent Peter out in search of supplies because her son-in-law Jim had telephoned earlier that morning and asked whether he and his two sons, Mavis and Peter's grandchildren, might come over and see them now that they were home, as the boys were desperate to see their grandparents again and tell them all about their Christmas. Mavis and Peter were equally desperate to see Jamie and Robbie, who were their recently deceased daughter's two children. Hannah and her family had relocated to Brighton, which was just under an hour's drive from her parents' home in Dorking, a year earlier, and then tragically she had been killed in a hit and run accident just a few weeks later. This had hit the entire family very hard, but as Adam's coping mechanism meant throwing himself into his work, he had only briefly returned home from New York for the funeral, and so he had not really spent any quality time with his young nephews in over a year. Mavis and Peter saw their grandchildren regularly. Their son-in-law Jim relied a lot on their help and support after losing Hannah, as whilst his family were more local to him, all living on the south coast of England as he now did, they didn't share the same sense of loss and grief. Whilst they'd loved Hannah, as she was the sort of person that everyone warmed to immediately, they had not known her nearly as well, and were far less able to answer the boys' questions and support them through their grief.

Peter returned shortly after Adam and Maddie arrived. He too was very pleased so see Maddie, but his general mood was not so great.

"Hardly anything was open" he explained as he passed a bag of groceries to his wife "and what I did find wasn't really that wonderful, but I traipsed round all over the place and I think I've managed to get everything you asked for love" he said. Mavis peered inside the bags.

"I see what you mean" she said, pulling out a cauliflower that looked somewhat the worse for wear. "Oh well, I'm sure I can do something with this. Are you okay with Cauliflower Cheese Maddie? The little lads love it and it was Hannah's favourite, so I usually make it if they're coming".

Maddie smiled as she replied. "I love it. What can I do to help Mavis?".

Lunch was almost ready when the doorbell rang. Considering that the family had all been away for a week and that Peter had struggled with the shopping, the feast Maddie and Mavis had cooked up between them was amazing. Peter answered the door to great shouts of "Grandad!" and "look what I got" then seconds later two bubbly boys burst through the kitchen door and launched themselves at Mavis "Nanna!".

Mavis hugged each of the boys tightly, whilst Peter introduced Maddie to Jim and then to the two boys. Maddie noticed that neither child had spoken to Adam. He had seemed so at ease with her various nieces and nephews the previous evening, yet his own nephews seemed uncertain around their uncle.

"Don't I get a hello then boys?" he'd asked, and they politely replied "Hello Uncle Adam" but they didn't really seem sure about conversing with him. There was obviously a lot of repair work needed in their relationship Maddie realised.

Jamie, Hannah and Jim's eldest child, was six years old. He was tall for his age, with dark brown hair, not dissimilar in colouring to Adam's and obviously followed the Baynes family in his looks Maddie realised, as he could have been a miniature version of Adam, who in turn looked very like his own father. Robbie, at four years old, was very different. He was small for his age, almost white blonde and very pale, much like his father who Maddie thought could only be about five and a half feet tall. Jim looked much older than the thirty-seven years Maddie knew him to be. Hannah's death had clearly taken its toll on her now rather haggard looking husband. His smile didn't quite reach his eyes and he had a haunted look about him. He was a lovely man, no doubt about that, and he was certainly very warm and caring towards his in-laws, but clearly hurting very much. Christmas had obviously been a very difficult time for him this year, and Maddie was sure that Mavis and Peter being in New York would have contributed to making it more difficult for Jim to bear. She silently vowed to help Adam repair these fractured relationships and also to support Jim, as he clearly needed help.

As the afternoon progressed, the boys seemed to relax more around Adam, although they were still clearly far more comfortable around their grandparents whom they saw regularly and obviously adored. Having seen several photographs of Hannah around the house, Maddie realised just how alike she and Mavis had been and knew that this must be a comfort to the boys, although maybe this made visiting more painful for Jim.

When the boys became restless, Maddie suggested that perhaps she and Adam could take them to a local park. Mavis, the jet lag now starting to hit her, thought this was a wonderful idea but Jim and Adam both seemed reticent.

"I'm great with kids" Maddie reassured Jim. "I look after my nieces and nephews all the time and they argue over who gets to be with Auntie Mads, which means I often end up surrounded by kids, so I can assure you that I'm capable of taking your two to the park for an hour or so". Adam had to admit that he'd seen first hand just how much the children at the party the previous evening had adored Maddie, and how good she had been with them all, but he was worried that he didn't really know these children and it was a huge responsibility looking after someone else's children.

"How about I go too" Peter suggested. "Fresh air will do me good and three adults to two children has to be a good ratio". Jim and Adam both visibly relaxed, and when the boys were offered the chance of a walk to the park with Grandad, both young boys jumped at the idea, so the five of them wrapped up warm and headed out to the park.

Maddie was like a big kid, on the swings and the slide with Jamie and racing him round the park. Robbie tried to copy, but he couldn't quite keep up.

"Help him Adam" Maddie shouted cheerily when she glanced backwards from the top of the slide and realised that whilst Jamie had climbed it easily ahead of her, Robbie was struggling behind. Adam was surprised when Robbie willingly clutched his hands as he offered assistance, and Peter stood back smiling and watching. He was fully aware of what Maddie was doing, actively encouraging Adam to play with his nephews. That was exactly why he hadn't rushed to Robbie's aid himself, as he would usually have done, and why he had stifled the potential of this outing not happening by volunteering to come too.

By the time they left the park, they were all exhausted. Jamie was hand in hand with Maddie as they walked through the gate and Adam was carrying Robbie who was now simply too tired to walk. In the space of just under and hour playing in the park, Maddie had managed to work miracles. Robbie now fully trusted his uncle, and was comfortable in his company, and whilst Jamie was not quite so demonstrative of his love for his uncle, Maddie had definitely won him round and he was even referring to her as "Mads" which was progress. Peter, it seemed, was surplus to requirements as they walked home, but this was a good thing he thought. This meant that the boys finally had more family support on the Baynes side of their family tree, and he could definitely see Maddie helping to fill a hole in their hearts.

3

Much as Maddie would have loved to stay and spend another night with Adam, she declined his suggestion of staying with him that evening and made the decision to travel home. Her two week break from work was coming to an end and she knew that the following morning her alarm would be ringing at a highly unsociable hour, and she still had lots to do in preparation for going back, not least trying to clear what she knew would be hundreds of work emails. She wasn't relishing the prospect of going back to reality, after what had been a mind blowing two weeks off, yet she knew that if she was going to pay the bills, she needed to earn her wage. She had the promise of a rather substantial inheritance coming her way within the next few weeks, but this would only keep her going for so long, particularly with all that she had planned for 2020, and therefore working for a living was still very necessary.

Promising Mavis and Peter that she would see them again very soon, and having made plans with Adam to meet him after she finished work the following day, she left the Baynes residence at the same time as the McDonald family. Both boys threw their arms around her waist as they said goodbye and she was pleased to see that, from Robbie at least, Adam received the same treatment. Even Jamie, more sceptical about his uncle's commitment to them, seemed to have relaxed around Adam and was willing to give him what could best be described as a half hug. Their father also seemed to have warmed to Maddie, kissing her on the cheek and thanking her for her help with the boys. This was progress, as whilst Jim had not exactly been unfriendly earlier, he was certainly wary of this stranger whom Adam had brought home. Maddie assured all three of them that they would be seeing her, and Adam, again very soon, and that she looked forward to being shown around Brighton Pier, which was apparently Jamie's favourite place in the whole wide world and somewhere he was desperate to introduce his new found friend to.

As Maddie drove back to Walton, she found herself once again replaying all the events of the past few days in her head. If someone had told her when she left work two weeks previously that she would be returning to work in a relationship, much less all the events which had led her to that stage, she would have laughed hysterically and most definitely would not have believed them. It all seemed too good to be true. There was also still an awful lot to decide, and a lot of obstacles which she and Adam needed to overcome. The only thing Maddie could be totally sure of was that none of it was going to be easy. Maddie had no idea how long Adam planned on being in the country, something she simply hadn't dared ask for fear of the answer, but she knew that whilst it was his intention to relocate to England permanently, sooner or later he would need to return to New York to make all the necessary arrangements. She was also realistic enough to know that this would take a considerable amount of time, which would mean them being apart for weeks on end, a prospect she was not relishing.

Pushing thoughts of Adam and his family to one side, Maddie mentally began preparing herself for the following two days at work, planning her outfits in her mind and creating a list of jobs in her head, as she knew that having been out for eight working days, there would be a lot of catching up required and she would have to prioritise certain tasks over others.

Adam, meanwhile, was explaining to Mavis and Peter the plans he had formulated on the aeroplane for the creation of a London based branch of the company he managed in New York. Neither of them fully understood everything that Adam was telling them, as he went into considerable detail, as if rehearsing his pitch to the Board with his parents, but they could see the spark of excitement blazing inside

Adam as he talked and Mavis realised that it was a very long time since she had seen her son quite so animated. She knew that his business was important to him, and that success in his career had been his sole goal in life until this point, but she also knew her son well enough to recognise that Maddie was the primary reason behind his excitement and enthusiasm and that the prospect of a new business venture was simply the metaphorical icing on the cake. Both Mavis and Peter voiced the concerns that Adam had anticipated, suggesting that whilst they would give him their full support no matter what path he chose, they were worried that starting a new business would be all consuming and defeat the primary object of his return to England, but he assured them both that he would be accountable to them for his actions from this point forward, and to Maddie too, and he would no longer be putting business first.

Later that evening, as Maddie curled up on the pillow that still smelt of Adam from the night before, and tried to switch her brain off enough to sleep, Adam lay in his childhood bed in his parents' house making plans. He texted Ed, whom he had met at Maddie's party the previous evening, because he thought reconnecting with someone quite prominent in the London business world would be beneficial, and arranged to meet him for lunch the following day. He then started a web search for properties to rent in the London suburbs. Part of him would love to move in with Maddie, but he knew that it was probably far too soon to suggest that, having known her less than a fortnight, no matter the intensity of their relationship, and equally he didn't feel he could impose on his parents indefinitely as they were used to having their own space, he and Hannah having both left home several years ago.

Aside from being surprised to find that she totally slept through the radio springing to life the following morning, and was therefore rudely awakened by the piercing bleeping of her mobile phone alarm, set as an emergency back up, Maddie's first day back was relatively uneventful. She arrived early as usual, partly to avoid the traffic, but mainly because she was super conscientious, and her worst fear was being late. She worked through her lunch break, grabbing a quick coffee and a takeaway sandwich from the staff canteen rather than having a proper break, and by 5.30pm she was more than ready to leave and stupidly excited at the prospect of heading home to meet Adam, who was due at her house an hour later.

Adam's day was just as busy and productive, but unlike Maddie, he had far more to report back. He had spent the morning with a local estate agent, viewing rental properties in Acton and Ealing and had not found anything which he really liked, but then he had met his former colleague Ed Smithers for lunch, and everything seemed to fall into place. Not only was Ed able to offer Adam some contacts who could support him in the start-up, and indeed Ed himself was keen on the idea of working with Adam in some form of partnership, but Ed also knew of a very swish two bedroom apartment which was available for rent in Canary Wharf. It had once belonged to Ed, then when he and Francesca were married and needed a bigger home, he had sold it to the tenant to whom he had previously let the property. That tenant was now in a similar position himself, getting married and moving away from the area into what he and his fiancé planned on being their family home, and therefore the place was once again available to rent. Like Adam's penthouse in New York, it had all the mod cons; huge American style fridge freezer, state of the art under floor heating, voice activated lights, remote control blinds and two large bedrooms overlooking the river Thames. It was exactly the sort of place where a career driven businessman would live, and it was available on a six month lease from the end of January. Adam had immediately decided that it was worth taking the plunge, had made an appointment to view it that afternoon, and minutes later, had signed on the dotted line. He was due to take possession of the keys on the 31st January.

As Adam told Maddie everything that had taken place throughout the day she felt a mild stab of disappointment that he felt the need to rent his own place, rather than asking to stay with her which is what she had thought he might do, but when he assured her that this would give them the best of both worlds for six months; the chance to be together in one or other abode for the majority of the time, but the ability to retreat to their own spaces if their relationship became too intense and they needed some time apart for a night or two, she knew he was right. She had initially imagined him staying with Mavis and Peter when he wasn't with her, but living with your parents when you are in your mid-forties isn't exactly a life goal, and lovely as their home was, it was a far cry from Adam's apartment in New York, as was her house come to that, and she wasn't sure he would really be happy giving up that lifestyle just yet, so renting a swanky flat in Canary Wharf did, indeed, seem like a sensible and practical plan. The fact that he was planning on getting the keys by the end of the month cheered her up too. She was certain he would need more time back in New York beyond the 31st January, and that it was highly unlikely that he'd become a permanent London resident again on that date, but it was certainly a move in the right direction and showed that he really was committed to the idea of returning home.

Maddie decided to broach the subject of when he might be heading back to America to make the necessary arrangements over there. Adam told her that he had managed to agree a meeting with the Board of Directors of his company on 10th January, which was just over one week away, and therefore he planned to return to the States the following Wednesday so that he could make preparations needed in advance of the meeting. He said that, all being well, he planned to return to the UK by the 29th January, so as to be in London to sign for the keys of his new apartment, but should there be a delay he had managed to agree that Ed could be his proxy. He suggested that perhaps Maddie might be able to take some more time off and return to New York with him, but she didn't feel that would be possible so soon after her previous trip, and he understood, knowing he would be extremely busy and unable to spend much time with her anyway.

As they ate leftover lasagne from the New Year's party, and discussed the logistics of the next few weeks, they both felt very positive. The first two days of the new decade had been both productive and enjoyable and for the first time in a very long time, both Adam and Maddie finally felt like the world was on their side.

4

Maddie found it very hard to leave the following morning, as Adam was still in bed and wasn't showing any signs of movement. She would have loved nothing more than to stay curled up beside him, but she was well aware that her boss had a big, important meeting that morning, and her presence, as his personal assistant, was very much required. Creeping around the house so as not to waken him, Maddie got herself ready for work.

Three coffees later, and leaving Adam sleeping soundly in her bed, Maddie penned a quick note to him with instructions on how to use the coffee machine, remembering his failed attempt on New Year's morning, and then headed out of the door. Whilst Maddie's mood was buoyant and full of hope and expectation, her boss, Anthony, seemed anything but and spent the morning snapping at Maddie for no reason in particular. This was very unlike Anthony and an uneasy feeling began growing in the pit of Maddie's stomach. Was there more to this meeting than she realised? Why was Anthony so uncharacteristically grouchy and why did everyone in the office seem heavy hearted? The previous day she had noticed that several of her colleagues seemed to be in a very sombre mood, but she refused to let that rub off on her and dampen her spirits. Today, however, the general demeanour of the office was bleak and although Maddie couldn't explain why, there was most definitely a feeling everywhere of impending doom.

Catching her friend Zoe on a rare trip to the ladies' loos, Maddie asked her how her Christmas had been. "Great thanks Mads, I just wish we hadn't come back to all this. Not the start any of us wanted to the New Year is it?". Maddie was bemused. There was obviously something going on that she was unaware of, and she needed to get back in the loop.

"I'm sorry Zo, but I have no idea what you're talking about. Everyone seems so down and depressed. What's happened?". Zoe looked at her friend, a shocked expression crossing her face.

"Do you really not know Maddie?" Zoe asked, somewhat incredulously, "I thought being Ant's PA you'd be the first to have heard the rumours. In fact, I have to admit that I was a little pissed off that you didn't tell me!". Maddie was confused. She had absolutely no idea what Zoe was talking about and told her as much.

"Apparently the meeting today is about a takeover. If it's all agreed, which looks likely, then chances are we're all surplus to requirements and out on our ears.". Now it was Maddie's turn to look shocked. She had been completely oblivious to the nature of the meeting, but if what Zoe had just told her was true, and she had no reason to doubt Zoe, especially as she was dating one of the senior managers and therefore often obtained inside information ahead of most of the workforce, then this made sense of Anthony's irrational rage and explained the bleak mood of her colleagues.

Maddie made her excuses and headed back to her little cubby hole in front of Anthony's larger, more impressive domain, just as he came out to demand yet more from her. Deciding that she'd been out of the loop for far too long, and seemingly having very little to lose at this point, Maddie bravely asked "Is it true?". Anthony's shoulders drooped and his head fell forwards slightly. His demeanour spoke for him. It was true.

Anthony looked like he had the weight of the world on his shoulders as he explained. "You know that profits have been down for the past couple of years?" Maddie nodded. She knew, from other Board meetings where she'd been the note taker, that the hotel chain was no longer as successful as it had been at the point she joined the company, but she also knew that several businesses were struggling in the current financial climate and had not been overly worried by the projections, as she believed the company to be relatively affluent. Apparently, this was not so.

"Business has been in decline for some time now and the bottom line is that we have run out of money and therefore out of chances. The owners have two choices. Sell out to one of the larger conglomerates or go bust. Obviously, while there's still assets that can be sold, they're going for option one, but chances of us keeping our jobs when the new lot takes over are slim. Non-existent in fact, if precedent is anything to go by. When this lot we're meeting with today bought out the Edwards hotel chain, they gave all their current employees just one hour to get up and clear out. I'm afraid it doesn't look good Maddie".

Maddie had absolutely no idea what to say. She was shocked. She had been completely oblivious to the financial state her employers were in and never once had she thought her job to be unsafe. Just as her life seemed to be taking an upturn, here was this massive blow. She couldn't afford not to be earning, even with her father's promised legacy, because she had a mortgage and bills to pay, not least the massive credit card debt she'd racked up in New York. It was fair to say that she didn't really want to leave either. Anthony was, with the exception of this morning when he was in a foul mood, understandably so she now thought, a great boss to work for; fair and appreciative. He was married with three young children too, so for him, losing his job would come as a particularly harsh blow because he was the only earner in the household. She hoped that he had been frugal with his money and had some savings tucked away to tide his family over. She didn't, but at least she only had herself to worry about and she knew that her family would never see her homeless or hungry, plus there was due to be a large sum of money coming her way within the next few weeks from her late father's estate. She would survive. Her thoughts were with those colleagues who wouldn't though, as she recognised that she was comparatively fortunate.

When Anthony emerged from the meeting at 2pm, Maddie had no need to ask how it went. His head hung low as he asked her to send a memo to all administrative staff inviting them to a meeting in the Board room at 2.30pm. In that meeting Anthony explained to all the gathered staff that Houlton Hotels had been bought out by a multinational company, and that their employment would be terminated with immediate effect. They would all receive a full month's pay in lieu of notice, but they were required to clear their desks by the end of the day and that from 4pm onwards, new personnel would be coming into the office to reset computer systems and take over their tasks. Anyone wishing to reapply for their job was welcome to do so, and the company would take into consideration their unblemished record with Houlton, but they would offer no guarantees of employment. Personnel on the 'coal face', those staff working in the hotels themselves, were safe for now, however new terms of employment would be issued to them shortly and their contracts reassessed over the forthcoming six months. Maddie looked around the room at her assembled colleagues. Some were quietly crying, others trying to look stoic, but all looked ashen and crestfallen. Part of her was pleased that she'd not known any of this until a few hours previously, as she knew that had she had an inkling of what might happen when she was in New York, she would have had a very different Christmas and New Year, but she was also ashamed not to have picked up on the sombre mood of her colleagues and asked questions sooner.

It felt very strange packing up her few personal possessions and leaving her office for the very last time that evening. It was even more of a wrench to say farewell to her colleagues, many of whom she knew it was unlikely she would ever see again. There were some she would stay in touch with, albeit only via social media, and some she would actively seek to maintain contact with, like Zoe, who she considered to be a friend as well as a workmate, but most of her colleagues were acquaintances that she chatted to in the office, and not people she was in any way invested in outside of work, and therefore the chances of maintaining any sort of contact beyond today were slim. Usually, when someone like that left the company, there was a leaving party; a chance to say a proper farewell. Today, however, no one was in the mood for a party, or even a drink at the local pub, and therefore each individual was simply packing up his or her belongings and slipping away quietly, no one wanting to be there when the new personnel arrived and not really wanting to say goodbye to their colleagues for fear of emotions getting the better of them.

Maddie was one of the last to leave the office. She still felt a sense of loyalty to Anthony, if not to the company, and he was obliged to remain in situ until his successors took over. Maddie therefore stayed, more for moral support than anything else, and helped him organise all his paperwork so that the handover would be smooth and fast. When they finally stepped outside into the cold, damp evening, Maddie couldn't help but wish there was something she could say to reassure Anthony, but all that came to mind was platitudes and she knew him well enough to know that these empty words would not be appreciated. Instead she simply thanked him for his support as an employer and wished him luck for the future, before they went their separate ways in the car park, to their own individual cars.

Initially, Maddie had intended to follow through with her plan to drive directly to Mavis and Peter's house, but an overwhelming sense of grief hit her as she started the engine and whilst she needed to get out of the car park and away from the building, she didn't want to drive very far at this point. She drove around the corner and into an industrial estate where she parked her car and sat, finally alone with her thoughts. She wanted to see Adam, to speak to him and explain that she was now suddenly unemployed, but she didn't want to have to be sociable, and who knew who else might be at his parents' house. She opted for a quick text instead.

"Had a shit day. Will tell all when I see you, but not up for socialising tonight. Please apologise to your parents for me and tell them I'll see them very soon. If you feel like coming to me later then great, but no worries if not. Love you. Xx"

Adam's reply was instantaneous.

"Sorry to hear that. Hope you're okay? I'll come to you as soon as Dad gets back with the car. Love you too. Xxx"

Maddie knew that he would be worrying about her, which was a nice thought, but she didn't feel she could elaborate more in a text so decided against a further response. Instead she started the engine and journeyed once again, heading in the direction of her beloved home, a home that thanks to her dad she might just get to keep hold of, because without his inheritance, she had no idea how she would pay the mortgage. She had lots of sums to do tonight.

5

By the time Adam pushed the doorbell to announce his arrival, Maddie was feeling more positive again. Her brother Josh had telephoned her whilst she was driving home from work to tell her the good news that probate had been granted earlier that day for their father's estate. This meant that the solicitors dealing with John Lane's affairs could now begin to release the funds to his beneficiaries. The solicitor had calculated that a sum of seventy four thousand, nine hundred and ninety eight pounds was due to each of John's four children, of which Maddie was one, and he would shortly be depositing the funds in each of their bank accounts. This was obviously a huge relief to Maddie, as whilst Radley had promised all Houlton employees one month's salary in lieu of notice, her January pay cheque would only pay her usual monthly bills, whereas this inheritance could, and indeed would, make a massive difference to her future.

A sum of money like that could be used in many ways, but Maddie had looked at all the possibilities and decided that if she paid £50000 off her mortgage when the renewal was up at the beginning of February, that should reduce her total monthly outgoings to around a thousand pounds per month. Once she had cleared her credit card, and paid for the holiday that she and her family had discussed a few days earlier, that would leave her enough money in the bank to survive for close to two years if she was frugal, and at least eighteen months if she wasn't. She was certain that she could find a suitable job in that time, even in the difficult financial climate the country was in at the moment, and worst case she could pick up some casual work as a caterer, or shop work to give her some extra spending money.

"Hey gorgeous" Adam said as Maddie opened the door to greet him, taking in her appearance with her freshly showered hair flung roughly into a ponytail, her sweatpants and comfy jumper and her big fluffy slippers. This was the most casual he had ever seen his girlfriend and whilst she really did look great in anything, he could tell from her lack of effort in her appearance that she had other things on her mind. As she closed the door behind them, he took her in his arms and wrapped her in a huge enveloping hug and held her tightly, without saying another word, correctly sensing somehow that she just needed his physical support. Eventually she broke their bond and gave him chance to remove his coat and shoes before escorting him into her lounge.

"Would you like a drink?" she asked, ever the hostess.

"No, I'm good thanks. What's up Mads? Your text had me worried".

Maddie explained about the Radley take over, being made redundant with immediate effect and the feeling of melancholy and indeed desperation she had witnessed amongst her colleagues that afternoon. "Wow" Adam said quietly as she finished recounting the events of her final day at work. "I'm so sorry Mads. What will you do? You know I'm here if you need anything, and I don't just mean metaphorically either. I've got money if you need a loan for bills and things". Maddie was grateful of his offer of support, but even if she had not had the promise of her father's inheritance, she could not have taken Adam's money as she didn't want their relationship to start with her being beholden to him. She explained about John's inheritance, and the happy coincidence of Josh's telephone call that evening, and how she had been looking carefully at all the options open to her financially.

Adam was in awe of her ability to bounce back and look on the bright side, despite the difficulties of the day. He also saw an opportunity in her lack of employment. "I know you said that you didn't want to be in debt to me so early in our relationship, and I get that, but how would you feel about me offering you a job, albeit temporarily?" he asked. Maddie looked inquisitively at him as he continued.

"You're an experienced personal assistant and I'm going to be juggling lots of balls in the air over the next few months, assuming that the start-up goes ahead. I've also got to manage the logistics of relocating from one continent to another, and that isn't going to be an easy task. Rosalie, my PA in New York, is fantastic, but I can't ask her to help with any of the London based work as apart from anything else, she's got young kids and won't be able to travel. You're here already and you know Ed. It looks like I'm going to be working very closely with after another meeting we had today, which I'll fill you in on later. I think you could be the perfect person to help me get things underway over here and it means that you have some form of employment to keep you going financially until you find whatever it is that you really want to do. What do you think?".

Initially Maddie was sceptical. She couldn't help but wonder whether Adam's job offer was really nepotism and based purely on a desire to support her, but as he went into more details about the conversations that he'd been having with Ed she realised that actually the need to employ a London based personal assistant was very real, and began to think that perhaps this could be the universe showing her the direction her new life would take. Adam and Ed planned on going into business together. Ed had made quite a name for himself in the London business world over the past twenty-five years and was now very successful and well respected, as Adam was in America. Adam's initial plan of bringing the Spruce Investments company name to the UK still stood in principle, but whereas previously Adam had envisaged the start-up needing significant funding from the Board of Directors in New York, Ed had now asked to invest. If Adam sold half of his shares in the New York branch to fund his share of the new branch of the company, still maintaining a large stake in the American side, and Ed invested fifty percent of the funds required, between them they would be co-owners and company directors, and would be able to finance the London based branch of the firm without support from the Board in America. All he needed was an investor in the States to purchase his US stock, and the approval of the Board to step down as CEO. If the Board was in agreement, then they would use the already well recognised name of Spruce Investments in the UK, as this would make the initiation easier, but if the Board were not willing to allow Adam to take the name with him, then he and Ed quite liked the idea of Smithers, Baynes and Co. as a company name.

The more she thought about it, the more Maddie liked the idea. It wasn't necessarily a long term solution, as working with your partner was fraught with difficulties, and working for your partner even more so, but as a temporary solution to her unemployment, and Ed and Adam needing someone that they could trust implicitly to support them in their new business venture, it was perfect. Maddie agreed to Adam's suggestion and he immediately telephoned Ed with the good news.

Maddie did have one request to make however, a request for time off in the school summer holidays. Maddie had yet to tell Adam about the plans that she and her family had made over their belated Christmas dinner the previous weekend. Maddie's younger sister was turning forty this year, and as both a means of celebrating that milestone birthday, and also honouring the memory of their parents, Maddie and all of her siblings and their respective families planned a trip to Disney World in Florida that coming summer. They had not yet booked anything, as they needed their inheritance money in order to fund the trip, but the plan was to hire villas in a village close to the Disney resort and to spend three weeks together in the sunny, magical kingdom. Not only did Maddie request a leave of absence during that time, but she also very much hoped that Adam would consider joining her. Adam jumped at the chance, explaining that he'd never been to Florida because his parents could never have afforded to take him and Hannah as children, much as they would have loved to, and then as an adult when he could easily afford to make the trip financially, he didn't feel it was an appropriate holiday for a single, childless adult male, even though he had always dreamed of going and been jealous of others who told him of their experiences.

Initially the plan had been for Maddie to share a villa with Juliet and her family, however thinking out loud as she and Adam discussed the holiday, another plan formed in her mind, and she voiced this to Adam.

"I completely understand if you don't think it's appropriate" she began, "but how about we extend the invitation to Jim and the boys, and your parents too come to that? I know that it's a huge extravagance, and I appreciate that Jim and your folks probably can't afford it, but from what you've said, I believe that you could easily afford to support them, and it would be such a wonderful thing for the boys to look forward to after having such a horrific year last year". Adam was quiet for a moment, thinking through the implications of what Maddie had just suggested.

"Are you sure Juliet and your brothers wouldn't mind us all crashing your family holiday?" he asked sceptically. "I'm sure the boys would love a trip to Florida, but adding that many extra people into the mix when you're already talking about three families plus us going together makes it an impossibly large group of people to accommodate".

Maddie wasn't deterred. "Florida is a big place and there's plenty of room for everyone. The beauty of us all going together is that we can share experiences when we want to, yet we can also be apart when we don't. It's much like you taking on that flat in Canary Wharf. It means we can all have our own space, yet also enjoy life together. What do you say?".

Adam said the only thing he could think of. "I'll talk to mum!".

6

Whilst Adam and Maddie were exploring potential options for their future in her house in Walton on Thames, just a few miles away in a much larger house in Hampton, a similar conversation was being held. Ed Smithers sat at the dinner table in the beautiful Edwardian home that he shared with his wife Francesca and their four children, outlining to Francesca and his father-in-law, the various plans that he and Adam had been making. Ed had stayed up in town the previous night, due to a New Year's corporate event that he was obliged to attend on behalf of his company, and therefore this was the first time he'd seen Francesca to explain his various meetings with Adam. He had waited until their meal was finished, and the children excused from the table, before broaching the subject with Francesca and her father Douggie Marten, who was a regular guest at their family meals.

Francesca honestly couldn't remember a time when her husband had seemed quite so motivated or animated.

"I've got my mojo back Ches" Ed explained. "I've been stuck in a rut at Charters for so long now, and sure it brings home the bucks, but it's not been a challenge for years and when the kids were small that was a good thing, because I needed to be here a lot more, but now, if I'm going to keep doing this job, I really need something that I can get my teeth into". Francesca remained quiet, studying her husband as he spoke.

"Just think of the future this could provide for the kids, darling. If me and Adam make a go of this, and we sure as hell intend to do just that, then they'll have a business to inherit one day. Bron's already planning to study business at university" he continued, referring to their sixteen year old daughter, "and if this takes off, she can come and work for the family firm. It will provide her with so many opportunities and it will be just the challenge that I need to see me through to retirement, by which time hopefully Bron, or one of the other kids, will want to take over the reins'.

Knowing that she had no right to stand in Ed's way, especially as he'd always been so supportive of her own career as a GP and senior partner in a local Heath Centre, and knowing that in the past ten years he had given up so much for her and literally put his own life on hold to accommodate the changes in their lifestyle that resulted from the tragic deaths of her best friend and adoptive sister Sally, and Sally's husband Tim, she felt guilty being so hesitant. When Sally and Tim had passed away, they discovered that Francesca was bequeathed guardianship of their two adorable, but very young daughters. At the time, Ed had only just come around to the idea of marriage, having proposed to Francesca just prior to the accident that claimed the lives of Sally and Tim. Having children was not something Ed had ever previously considered, yet despite the concept of fatherhood being completely alien to him, very soon he had moved in with Francesca to help her bring up the girls and later, after the couple had married, she and Ed had officially adopted Bronwyn and her younger sister Libby, both of whom were loved just as much as the two boys that were later born of their union. In the space of a year, Ed had transformed from a high flying bachelor boy businessman, into a domesticated husband and father, and she would be eternally grateful for his unending support, especially everything that he had done for her family during that horrific year. Francesca wanted to return that support now, and to encourage her husband in this venture that clearly excited him and ignited a passion in him that she had not seen for many years, if ever, yet she was sceptical about how it would impact on their family, and the welfare of their children always had been, and would remain, her first priority.

"You say that the capital for this project would come from the sale of stock you already hold, and you wouldn't need to use the house as security?" she asked, this being her biggest fear. "I don't want to stand in your way, but I couldn't agree to this if there was a chance that we could lose our home".

Ed's reply was instant and vehement "Of course. You know that I'd never do anything to jeopardise our home, or the kids' futures" Ed assured his wife. "There is a reason I was determined to be mortgage free on this place as soon as humanly possible" he continued "because I want to be certain that no matter what happens, Bronwyn, Libby, Doug and Danny will always have a roof over their heads and food on the table. I would never in a million years do anything to put the security of our family at risk".

Francesca knew this to be true, and also knew that whilst he may not be as excited by business as he once was, Ed was certainly good at what he did, and his astute investments over the years had not only paid off their mortgage on the large five bedroom house they had lived in for the past ten years, but his success in business had also enabled her to buy out her former colleague Derek's share of the practice when he retired, without the need to borrow from the equity in their home. She also knew that he had a very healthy portfolio of stocks and shares which provided a rich and regular additional income to pay for holidays and other luxuries, but she couldn't help wondering how selling these would affect their lifestyle.

As if reading her mind, Ed went on to explain that as buying into this venture with Adam would require liquidising most of his assets. They might have to cut back a little on holidays in the interim period until the business was up and running, or pay for them with Francesca's salary which was currently being used to put money in trust for their children's futures, but that otherwise there would be no discernible difference to their lifestyle.

"I might have to work longer hours again for a while, just while we get on our feet so to speak, but once we're established, we can start to employ a workforce and hopefully in the long run that will mean that I can cut back on my hours again and spend more time with you and the kids". Francesca was well aware that many of Ed's colleagues, just as he himself once had, worked minimum fourteen hour days and often six or even seven days per week. Ed, being a family man, always endeavoured to be home in time for dinner with the family, or at the very least before the children went to bed at night, and on the rare occasions when that wasn't possible, such as the previous night when he was obligated to attend a function in the City, he always video called them to say goodnight. He rarely ever worked weekends now, and thanks to a couple of young and childless GPs in the practice, who were happy to earn the extra money at weekends, the same was also true of Francesca, but they still relied heavily on her father for support with childcare, which was the main reason that Douggie was here with them now.

"I think you should go for it, son" Douggie encouraged, showing support for the man whom he had come to truly love and admire over the past ten years. "As the three of us know all too well, life is far too short to miss out on fantastic opportunities, and this sounds like something that you really want to do?" Ed nodded in response to the older man's questioning tone. "In my view, for what little it's worth, if that's the case, and so long as you're sure it's not too risky, I think you should take the chance while you can".

Francesca just had one more question before she could agree with her father and give her husband's proposal her blessing. "How well do you know Adam?" she asked. "Obviously I only met him briefly for the first time on Tuesday night" she continued, "but he seems very impulsive to me, I mean, he literally only met Maddie two weeks ago, and in that time he claims to have fallen in love with her and is uprooting his entire life to move to England, just so that he can be with her. It just seems very sudden. Are you really sure that going into business with someone who acts on a whim is safe?".

Ed laughed, and reached across the table to give his wife's hand a reassuring squeeze. "When you put it like that, I can completely understand your concern, but honestly, the impulsiveness is totally out of character, and let's face it, we all do crazy things for love" he smiled at his wife, referring to him totally uprooting his own life when she had taken on the guardianship of the girls in order to be there to support her.

"I've known Adam since way back in the day, and our paths have crossed quite a few times over the years. He's a couple of years older than me, and when I was starting out in the business world, he and some girl called Sophie something-or-other were the hottest news in town. They showed massive potential and companies were literally clambering to get the pair of them on their payroll. She disappeared off the radar a few years later, but Adam seemed to go from strength to strength. He was continually head-hunted, made some amazing investments, and consequently wound up as CEO of Spruce Investments based in New York. His name has huge power in the business world and I'm positive that between the two of us, we can make a real success of this. I'm not saying it will be easy Ches, in fact I know it's going to be bloody hard work and going to take a hell of a lot of determination and guts to get this idea off the ground, but I really want to do this because for the first time in years, I'm truly excited about work again. I know it might seem like some kind of midlife crisis, and maybe to a certain extent it is, but I promise you that if you agree to this, I won't let you down. Please say you'll support me Ches?".

Ed's plea was enough for Francesca. His reassurances about Adam helped too, and she suggested that he invite Adam and Maddie over for lunch on Sunday so that they could all get to know each other better and discuss the logistics together, to which Ed immediately agreed. He thanked both Douggie and his wife for their support and headed off into the lounge to make the telephone call to Adam.

"Do you really think we're doing the right thing here Dad?" Francesca asked her father, clarifying "It's one hell of a risk that Ed wants to take, because if the business doesn't work and we lose all that capital he has invested then what future will the kids have?".

Now it was Douggie's turn to squeeze her arm reassuringly. "You'll still have love Ches, and you'll have the kids and your family, and this house. Besides, with your earnings from the surgery, and all that you've stashed away for the children's futures, you're not exactly going to be broke even if Ed loses every penny he invests. I think this is the right thing for Ed, I think he needs to do this, and I honestly think it will be good for your relationship too. You saw how animated he was and how excited he is about this. When was the last time you saw him so buoyed up, hey? I don't think I've seen him like this since your wedding day Ches. Trust him. He's never let you down before, and whilst I can see that lots of things are going to change in the coming months, something tells me that he's more devoted to you and the kids than ever. He'll make this work, because he's doing it to try and make an even better life for all of you". At her father's wise words, Francesca smiled. Ed truly was one in a million, and Douggie was right. She needed to let Ed do this, because this was his passion.

7

On Saturday morning, Maddie suggested to Adam that they should visit Jim and the children in Brighton and suggest the idea of Florida to him. Adam still wasn't entirely convinced about inviting his family to join them, but did agree that it would serve to strengthen the relationship he was rebuilding with his family if they made the drive to the coast. Collecting Mavis and Peter on the way, they explained to the older couple why Maddie had not wanted to socialise the previous evening and broached the subject of a family holiday in Florida.

Initially, the plan was met with some trepidation, as Adam had anticipated. They appreciated the gesture, but having experienced an eight hour flight to New York the previous week, the idea of another long haul flight so soon didn't exactly appeal to them, but when Maddie explained why she had wanted to invite them, Mavis seemed to waver a little.

"I know it's a big deal for you to go all that way, and I realise that theme parks probably aren't your thing, but there are lots of other things you can do. The outlet malls are fantastic for shopping, and there's the Kennedy Space Station which Peter you will absolutely love, and you can go on cruises to see alligators and so much more. My sister, Juliet, suggested that we do this as a family both to celebrate her fortieth birthday, but also to commemorate my dad's life and honour his memory by spending a portion of his legacy travelling together as a family. I know that you guys never knew my dad, and haven't even met the rest of the brood yet, but I thought it would be a lovely treat for the boys and Adam said it was somewhere he and Hannah always wanted to go as kids, so you could come in her memory and the trip could be about making new happy family memories for all of us. You and Peter could share a villa with me and Adam, and then Jim and the boys could have another one and each of my siblings would have a villa with their respective families. We could do things all together when we wanted to, but also spend time on our own when it was appropriate. Please at least think about it" she pleaded.

Mavis was torn. She loved the idea of spending three weeks with Adam, Maddie, Jim and the boys, but she was still hesitant about the flight and also the cost. "If we come, I wouldn't feel comfortable with you paying Adam, especially as you're about to start a new business and have all the expense that comes with that. We have some savings, don't we Peter?" she asked, as her husband nodded enthusiastically "and we could probably afford to pay for Jim and the children too".

Maddie smiled. Mavis was clearly warming to the idea. "What about you Peter, what do you think?" she asked Adam's father.

"To be honest love, I've always wanted to go to Florida, but since we've had the cash, it's not really been appropriate to go. The idea of going to NASA is a massive selling point for me, and I might be getting on a bit, but you're never too old for the odd rollercoaster, and I hear that the ones out there make the Big One in Blackpool pale into insignificance. If Jim and the kids are up for it, and if Mavis is happy, then I'm in".

Hearing the enthusiasm in Peter's voice as he spoke was Mavis' undoing. "You really want to go, don't you?" she asked. Peter nodded once again and looked at her with what Maddie could only describe as pleading eyes. "Okay then" Mavis acquiesced. If Jim agrees, then we'll go!". Maddie literally cheered as she continued to drive them all down the M23.

Jim, it transpired, was more difficult to convince. It wasn't that he didn't want to go to Florida, for it was indeed somewhere that he and Hannah had always planned to take the boys once they were at an age when they would appreciate it, but, as Maddie had correctly guessed when she'd first met him, he was wary of this newcomer in their lives and also still very much struggling with his grief, which made making big decisions uncomfortable. Adam was actually the one to talk him round, saying that he wished he'd had the forethought to suggest a family trip to Florida whilst Hannah was still alive, knowing that he could easily have afforded to treat them all, yet he'd been too selfish and wrapped up in work to make that offer. Now, having had his eyes opened to the importance of family, and determined to make changes to his lifestyle, he didn't want to live with regret. That meant doing things like this in Hannah's memory. He then recounted his experiences at the Rockefeller ice rink, where it took numerous attempts and Maddie's unrelenting patience to finally get him on the ice and skating as he'd once promised his sister that he would. Nothing could bring Hannah back to them, but they could work together as a family to keep her memory alive for her sons.

When they broke the news to the boys, they were absolutely over the moon. Jamie's best friend had been to Disney World the previous summer and had come back to school in September raving about his experiences. With Maddie's help, he was online on his dad's laptop investigating all the different parks and deciding exactly what he wanted to see and do. Robbie, being that much younger, didn't fully understand anything more than that he and his dad and brother were going on a holiday with his grandparents and uncle, but having vague memories of his last family holiday in Cyprus, a few months before his mum passed away, and remembering splashing in the swimming pool and dancing on stage with a large penguin, he too was swept up in the excitement, and when he found out that he would get to meet Mickey Mouse and lots of other Disney characters, he was absolutely elated.

After lunch in a chip shop on the sea front, having declared it too cold and windy to get a takeaway to eat on the beach, the extended family made their way onto Brighton Pier. Jamie was in his element, showing Maddie and Adam all of his favourite attractions and Robbie happily bobbed along with him, telling anyone who would listen that they were all going to go on holiday and meet Mickey Mouse. Mavis tried to explain to him that they were not going until the summer holidays, but although as a rising five he had started school the previous September, he had no concept of when the long break would actually come.

When they went down to walk on the beach, the boys wanting to paddle in the very edge of the sea in their wellington boots, Mavis took hold of Maddie's arm and hooked hers through it.

"Thank you, my dear" she whispered quietly, close to Maddie's ear, although the menfolk were now splashing around with the boys by the water's edge, so out of ear-shot by this point.

"Whatever for?" Maddie asked, somewhat surprised by Mavis' actions, as she didn't feel that she had done anything in particular for the older lady that day, having focused her attentions on the young boys.

"For this" Mavis replied, gesticulating with her free arm towards her family playing on the beach, "for giving me the chance to spend time with all of my family together and for encouraging Adam to come back to us all. You have no idea how grateful I am, and I'm sorry if I was reticent about the idea of Florida, when I now truly understand why you suggested it, but at first I was worried that it might be another example of Adam trying to buy our affections, rather than genuinely wanting to spend time with us. Now I know that I was wrong, and I know that thanks to you, there will be many more days like this, where Adam spends time with those boys and really gets to know them again. Peter and I had almost given up hope that this would ever happen, yet here we are, and it's because of you".

Maddie smiled. Family was very important to her, and she could never imagine being parted from her own family for any length of time, so she still didn't fully understand what had made Adam distance himself so much in recent years. The physical distance was obvious, because his job had required him to live in New York, which clearly made it difficult for him to see his family regularly, but the reason for placing such emotional distance between them as well, was something she still intended to uncover. She truly hoped that once she'd helped him to heal the relationships and rebuild the trust he needed to have with his family, that she would be able to determine what had really made him shut himself away from them all. Either way, she was adamant that from this point forward, he would be a loving son, brother-in-law and uncle and she would hold him accountable for any decisions that he made which proved detrimental to that.

As Maddie drove Adam and his parents back to Surrey, the mood in the car was bright. They were only a few days into the year, yet so much had already happened and so many changes had been made. The new decade marked the beginning of a new future for the Baynes family, and that future included Maddie too, which thrilled her to the core. She loved her family dearly but had always been slightly jealous that she didn't have a partner of her own, someone with whom she could potentially have children and build her own branch of the family, just as each of her siblings had done. It was as if they were part of an exclusive club, from which she was barred. Now, finally, she felt that she also belonged to that club because she had Adam, and she had his family, and she had the promise of a very challenging, but equally exciting, year ahead.

8

"Danny will you please stop eating the carrots darling, I'm trying to get dinner ready and you boys are eating them as fast as I can peel and chop them". Francesca was feeling haggard. Normally her sons pinching food from the kitchen wouldn't bother her in the slightest, but right now it was the source of additional stress. Ridiculous really, but she hadn't been sleeping particularly well recently, especially since Ed had spoken to her about the idea of going into business with Adam, and things which wouldn't normally faze her were getting to her more than they should. She was moody and irritable, and she couldn't quite place her finger on why. Perhaps it was the menopause she thought. Whatever the reason, she knew she had to snap out of it, or at the very least find more patience with the children.

Francesca fully understood why Ed wanted to do this, and more than anything she wanted to support her husband, with whom she was very much in love, but the idea of sinking all their future nest egg into a new business venture sounded like too big a risk to her and she was worried. She also had stress to deal with at work, as one of her most trusted GPs had just gone on maternity leave, which was great news for Julia, but meant that Francesca's workload had increased as the newly trained registrar who was covering needed far more support than the highly experienced GP she was replacing.

Ed, meanwhile, was in seventh heaven. He had spent all weekend making plans. He had revelled in the opportunity to explain to his eldest daughter Bronwyn all the intricacies of what he and Adam planned to do; how they would fund it, the promotion strategy, what the business would entail and she had soaked up every last detail. Francesca could definitely see the sixteen year old joining Ed in the business world in the near future. She was already quite the young entrepreneur, having started up her own little business creating and selling revision materials to other students. It had started when she'd posted her GCSE books for sale online after finishing her exams. Someone had bought one of them and seen the really detailed revision notes that she'd included in the package. Impressed by these, the buyer had emailed and asked whether she had any more notes of the same ilk, and all of a sudden, Bron was emailing out her own personalised 'Bronwyn Childs-Smithers GCSE Revision Quick Guides' all over the place and making a nice little sum of money in return. She was only one term into her A levels at college, yet had already started making A Level guides too. This girl definitely had a head for business, thought Francesca, and her adoptive dad's new venture thrilled her just as much as it did him. If only she, as wife and mother, could share their enthusiasm.

"Mum, please would you help me with this science homework?" Francesca's thoughts were interrupted by Libby, her fourteen year old daughter who was, in complete contrast to her sister, only really interested in the arts. It wasn't that Libby didn't try hard at school, she really did, but she was finding Year 10 impossibly difficult, even with the support of Bronwyn's revision guides, and she often needed help with her homework, unless of course it was Music, or Art. Even her GCSE PE homework often resulted in Francesca sitting with her and helping her to understand the biology aspect, as although she was relatively good at the practical, the theory side bemused her completely. Once Francesca had been called to the school because one of her teachers felt that Libby's apparent lack of knowledge and inability to remember academic facts had been a deliberate attempt to avoid the work, but then when Francesca had explained just how dedicated she was, and how much help she needed to complete her homework, they had run some tests and found that she had a processing difficulty which made academic learning incredibly difficult for her. This should have been picked up sooner, but in Primary School, where she had the same teacher all day and every day, the teacher had seen the effort she put in to her studies and wasn't worried about her, whereas once she was at secondary school, some of the teachers began to perceive her as lazy and not trying, because they only saw her for an hour or two each week and didn't recognise the effort she was putting into different tasks. Now she had a special support plan called an EHCP which meant she received help from the Special Needs department in her school and she was doing much better, but at home that same help was also required.

"I'm sorry Lib" said Francesca, "I'm in the middle of preparing lunch at the moment and I can't really stop now as they're due here in an hour, but I'm sure if you ask your sister she could help you, or if you leave it until after Maddie and Adam have gone, I can help you later". Any other child, particularly a teenage girl, might have been upset by not being first priority at that moment, but not happy and bubbly Libby whose reply was totally in character for the girl

"Okay Mum, no worries, would you like me to help you with lunch?".

By the time Maddie and Adam arrived at the large, five bedroomed Edwardian house in Hampton, the aroma of roast lamb filled the house and the food was almost ready. Welcoming them in, Francesca hugged Maddie warmly, having got to know her very well over the years as she was one of her sister-in-law Fiona's oldest, closest friends, and then shook Adam's hand. Ed immediately took Adam off to get him a drink and Maddie followed Francesca into the kitchen where she helped with the final dishing up and serving of dinner. The chatter over the table at lunchtime was very jovial. Francesca wanted to hear all about Maddie's holiday in New York, and the children were excited to tell Maddie all about the gifts they had received at Christmas. It was only as the meal neared its end, and the youngest three children were excused to do other things, that the conversation turned to the new business venture.

Francesca watched everyone sitting around her large dining table talking animatedly. She could completely understand why Adam and Ed got on so well, as they clearly had a lot in common, and not just their business acumen. They were very alike in a lot of ways, dedicated to success, but also passionate about making a difference and it had become clear earlier in the meal that Adam's return to the UK had as much to do with his family circumstances as it did with Maddie, which reassured Francesca somewhat as it meant he also prioritised those whom he loved. Francesca was happy for Maddie too. In all the years she'd known Maddie, she'd never seen her look quite so alive as she did now. She was apparently going to become Adam's personal assistant, for the time being at least, a role which, had Bron been a few years older, she would have loved to take on for Ed. Who knew; maybe she would in the future. Maddie seemed radiant. Considering she'd lost has job two days previously, and had a very traumatic year in 2019, she was incredibly buoyant. Love clearly suited her, and whilst Francesca wasn't entirely sure she believed in love at first sight, it was obvious that Maddie and Adam were already very much in love and she wished them every happiness.

"So, I've been thinking a lot this weekend" said Ed, looking over in Bronwyn's direction, "and with the support of my business advisor here, I've got a suggestion to make. I know that plan A was to take on the established Spruce name, and to use that for our business over here so that we could trade off its success, but the more I've thought about it, and the more we've discussed it…"

"… You think Smithers, Baynes and Co would be a better option" Adam finished for him.

"Yes" Ed agreed. "Yes, I do".

Adam laughed. "Mads and I said the same thing. The more we've discussed this over the past forty eight hours, the more I think I need to cut ties with Spruce. I'll keep whatever shares I can afford to, and I'm sure that you plan to keep a few from other companies in your portfolio too, but I think that rather than going at this as a UK branch of Spruce, we should set up as a brand new entity, where we're only answerable to each other in that first instance".

Ed nodded. "Couldn't agree more, mate. Definitely the direction we should take, after all, in the business world, you and I are potentially as well known as Spruce is, certainly in this country, so I say we trade off ourselves rather than another company".

Wine flowed and the conversations continued. Francesca didn't feel quite as uneasy now as she had earlier, feeling reassured that Adam was as committed to this venture as her own husband was, but she still had reservations about the amount of time Ed would need to spend on this, and the fact that he was sinking an awful lot of money into one business. The advantage of his current share portfolio was that he had shares in numerous different companies based all over the world. If one of those were to fail, there would be a loss, but it wouldn't be catastrophic because he would still have a substantial amount invested elsewhere. That wouldn't be the case if everything he had was invested in Smithers, Baynes and Co. but perhaps she was worrying unnecessarily.

Maddie couldn't help but notice Francesca looking withdrawn. As she helped her clear the table she asked quietly "Are you okay Ches? You don't look yourself and at a guess I'd say you're not exactly enthused by all this?". Francesca was ashamed to have been caught doubting and quickly brushed off Maddie's concern.

"Sorry Mads, I'm okay, honestly. It's just that I'm tired after a manic Christmas and all that. I'm really happy for Ed that he's got this venture to sink his teeth into and I know he's thrilled to bits about working with Adam. I don't mean to put a dampener on things, it's just that I don't really understand business and I find it hard to get excited by it, but I'm behind them on this, really I am". Maddie was less than convinced, but decided not to push the issue, instead changing the subject and telling Francesca all about her family's plans for a holiday of a lifetime in the summer. Little did Maddie realise, but this was the last thing Francesca wanted to talk about, as the thought of not being able to afford a holiday like that this year, only served to dampen Francesca's mood further! Boy, I really do have the January blues this year, thought Francesca to herself.

9

Considering that neither of them had work to go to on the Monday morning, both Adam and Maddie were up and dressed very early in the morning, more out of habit than necessity.

"What would you like to do today? Adam asked Maddie, knowing that they were both the type of people who needed to stay occupied, yet having no clue what to actually do himself.

"How about we play at being London tourists today?" she suggested. "We've ticked off lots of the tourist attractions in New York recently, and I realised the other day when I was in town with Fiona, that there are so many things I've never done which I'd love to do, like go on the London Eye and visit the Tower of London. What do you say?" she asked.

"Sounds perfect" Adam replied.

The trains were surprisingly quiet, considering that it was technically still commuting time when they boarded the train bound for Waterloo station, and by 9am they were in Central London and heading across the South Bank towards the London Eye. As it was still so early, and a Monday morning at that, there was literally no queue for the famed attraction and therefore they were able to secure a pod all to themselves. The views really were spectacular, it being a crisp and clear day, and they used the tablets installed in their pod to identify different areas and landmarks in the city. Having completed their ride on the Eye, they headed across Westminster Bridge towards St James' Park, which they walked through to get to Buckingham Palace, stopping to take selfies in front of Big Ben and the Queen's London residence. Walking across the Mall to Trafalgar Square, Maddie suggested it was time for brunch, and being a lover of Art, the National Gallery coffee shop seemed the perfect place to sit for a few moments and recharge, before exploring the exhibits held within the gallery.

By the time they got to the Tower of London, it was mid-afternoon. They'd walked around Covent Garden and visited St Paul's Cathedral, then after another quick pit stop at a nearby café, they'd caught the tube to Tower Bridge. Their tour of the Tower, guided by a Yeoman Warder, was fantastic. The beefeater guiding them was full of tales of the history of the tower and its previous incumbents, explaining the various imprisonments and executions which had taken place in the tower. They also got to view the amazing crown jewels and armoury dating back hundreds of years.

Finishing their day with an Italian meal in Leicester Square, they returned to Maddie's house that evening exhausted, but having had a very enjoyable day.

"Thank you for today" Maddie said, as she handed Adam a glass of wine and curled up next to him on the sofa.

"Thank you too" he replied earnestly. "I had a wonderful day".

Maddie smiled. It really had been lovely, and she felt incredibly lucky to have this man by her side. "I know the next few months are going to be manic, particularly with launching the new business" she said, "but let's make a vow now to have a date day like that at least once a month. It can be our day for not thinking about anything or anyone else but us". Adam agreed that it was a great idea, and they began to discuss all the things that they would like to do on future date days.

Maddie wasn't sure that she wanted to spoil the mood, especially as she was the one to suggest that date days like today should be about nothing other than them, but she also knew that they couldn't avoid the practicalities for much longer.

"We really need to talk about what's going to happen over the next few weeks" she began, broaching the subject. "I know there's going to be things that crop up which we can't plan for, but if I'm going to be looking after things here for you whilst you're back in New York, then we need to know which of us is supposed to be doing what and come up with a suitable schedule".

Adam thought this would be a good time to suggest something that he'd been mulling over since she lost her job. "How would you feel about coming back to New York with me next week?" he asked. "I know you declined when I first suggested it because you couldn't take the time off work, but I was thinking that if you could come back with me, even for just a week or so, you could meet Rosalie, who is my PA in New York, and she can give you the run down on how the business works and what she does, and then while I'm wrapping things up on the business side, you could help with sorting out the apartment and things like that. We can't really move forward with the London business until I've formally resigned and liquidised my shares in Spruce, or until Ed has raised his share of the funds, so we're kind of in limbo here, but there's plenty to do over there. What do you say?"

Maddie was torn. She loved New York, and liked the idea of going back, but she really couldn't justify spending money on flights at the moment and didn't really want Adam paying her way. She voiced these concerns and he immediately brushed them away.

"You wouldn't be coming for a holiday though, that's the whole point. You'd be coming as my PA, and working for me while you're there, so you'd travel as my assistant. Obviously, accommodation wouldn't be a problem because, as my girlfriend, you'd stay with me, although I could put you up in a hotel close to the office if you'd prefer, but you'd have plenty of work to do. It won't be a jolly like at Christmas. Please say you'll come. I really don't want to go back without you".

Maddie thought for a while and then asked him "So what exactly do you envisage me doing in New York?".

Adam explained that her first priority, after obtaining information on his business dealings and working habits from Rosalie, whom he thought she should spend a few days shadowing, would be meeting realtors on his behalf and deciding what to do with his penthouse.

"If anyone can stage that place for sale or rental, it's you" he commented, referring to the way she had transformed it from gadget central to homely apartment two weeks previously, finishing only moments before his parents had visited at Christmas and allowing them to believe, at least until he admitted the truth a few days later, that their son had lived with these home comforts for the duration of his three years in the City.

"I don't know whether to sell or to put the place up for rent, and I guess to a certain extent that depends on how much interest I keep in Spruce, but either way, we need to get figures from an agent as to what income the property will obtain and we need to prepare it for viewings, as one thing is certain, I won't be living in it for much longer". Maddie smiled. She had loved decorating Adam's apartment for Christmas, adding lots of more homely touches to make it more welcoming for his parents' visit, and she could certainly see herself staging it ready for prospective buyers or tenants to view it.

"Okay" she said finally, "I'll come back to New York with you, but you must give me jobs to do; use me as your assistant. If you don't, then I'm coming back here and looking for paid work of my own. Deal?".

Adam was thrilled. "Deal!" he exclaimed, kissing her soundly on the lips. "I'm so pleased that you'll be with me. I don't think I'll ever be happy on my own in New York again." She laughed at him. This was the man who, for three years, had been so happy in his own little world on the other side of the Atlantic that he'd rarely ever returned home and yet now, little more than two weeks after their first meeting, here he was telling her that he didn't believe he could be there on his own ever again.

"You're just a hopeless romantic at heart, aren't you?" she teased.

"I could show you just how romantic I am if you like?" he said seductively, leaning in close and nudging her nose with his.

"You could, but don't you have flights to organise for your new PA?" she countered, purposefully getting up and retrieving her laptop from the other side of the room which she passed to him.

"If we're flying out on Wednesday, like you said you were, then there's a lot to do in the next 24 hours, not least giving this place a good old clean because there's no way I'm leaving it in it's post Christmas state until I get home'. The previous evening, upon returning from Ed and Francesca's house, they had taken down all of Maddie's extensive collection of Christmas decorations, because upon realising that it was twelfth night and unlucky to leave them up any longer, Maddie had insisted on the job being done, but whereas she would usually give the house a thorough clean once the decorations were stashed away for another year, she hadn't felt hoovering at midnight would go down well with the neighbours, so had decided to leave that for another day.

"Mads, it's eleven thirty in the evening. Surely you're not considering cleaning now?" Adam asked, worried at what his girlfriend might be asking of him, as he was truly shattered and only really in the mood for sleeping by this point.

"No, but I do intend to get up early tomorrow and get on it, so right now I'm going to fix us a nightcap whilst you book my ticket, then we're going to 'climb those wooden hills to Bedfordshire' as my grandad used to say, and get a decent night's sleep in preparation for all that we need to do tomorrow".

Adam managed to secure another first-class ticket on his flight on the Wednesday morning, and paid for it on his AMEX card, then sent a quick text to his parents to update them on everything, before following Maddie up the stairs to bed.

10

Two weeks prior to Christmas, like many of her patients, all four of Francesca's children plus her husband and father, had succumbed to the norovirus which seemed to be sweeping through households like wildfire. It had started with Danny, who, like most of the other children in reception class, started vomiting in the middle of the night, then by morning little Doug had also looked peaky and so Francesca decided it was safest to keep him off school, and sure enough, by midday he was also poorly. Libby had then started throwing up just as Danny began to perk up and then both Bronwyn and Ed had been afflicted by the weekend, as had Douggie senior, who had been helping Francesca with caring for the children. Miraculously, she had escaped, or so she thought at the time, but now, curled up on the floor of the en suite bathroom that she and Ed shared, hugging the toilet bowl which she had vomited into at least three times in the past hour, she wondered if this was a delayed reaction, or the start of another round of illness for the family.

Ed was brilliant, organising the children for school and making himself late for work in the process, but she knew that he couldn't stay any longer.

"I'm so sorry darling" he said as he rubbed gentle circles on her spine with one hand and held her hair back for her with the other, as yet another wave of nausea hit her. "If I could stay then I would, but I'm the one who's called this meeting at 9.30am and I really can't miss it".

She fully understood. This meeting was with some clients that Ed hoped would follow him into the new business venture with Adam and therefore particularly important to him. He'd talked about it all the previous evening. She knew that he had to go, and to be honest, whilst she fully appreciated his support, part of her just wanted to be left alone to be poorly in peace anyway.

"I've called Sandi" he told her, referring to the practice manager at the surgery where Francesca was the senior partner, "and I've told her that you won't be in today and she says not to worry and that she'll sort everything. Your dad knows too, and he'll collect the kids from school as usual and bring them home. He says to call him if you need anything before that. I'll drop the boys at breakfast club on my way out, and the girls can get the bus today. You just focus on getting well. I love you" he finished, kissing her gently on the top of her head.

A brief nod was all she could manage in response as once more a wave of vomiting overtook her body. She could sense that Ed didn't want to leave her, but also knew he must get the kids out of the way. Reluctantly he stood, as the vomiting passed, and she gave him a small wave and the best smile her exhausted body could muster.

By some miracle, the last bout of vomiting that she suffered as Ed and the children left the house, seemed to be it, and after a few hours in bed recovering, she woke up feeling absolutely fine and also starving hungry. Deciding not to risk anything too rich, she opted for a slice of toast and a glass of water. Surprisingly, she held both down with no problems and curled up in front of the television to watch a movie which she'd recorded over Christmas and never quite got around to watching. By 1pm she felt completely normal again and decided to risk eating a sandwich and drinking a cup of herbal tea, both of which also seemed to stay put in her stomach and not cause her to run for the bathroom. She texted Ed to tell him the good news, then phoned Sandi to check on everything at work.

"Don't worry Ches, it's all in hand. I've managed to move most of your patients to the other doctors as everyone had plenty of gaps so we didn't need a locum for today and Mark has said he'll happily work some overtime tonight to ensure that all the emergency patients get seen too, so we're absolutely fine. You just concentrate on getting well. It's not like you to be sick". It really was unusual for Francesca to contract any illness. She seemed to have an immune system made of steel that nothing could penetrate. It didn't seem to matter what ailments her patients presented with, or what bugs the kids picked up at school, she was someone who always seemed to avoid contracting them.

"Well thank you Sandi" Francesca replied. "All being well, I should be back to normal tomorrow. I know the rules are that you should quarantine yourself for forty eight hours after a bug, but I feel so normal now that I'm beginning to think it must have been something that I ate instead. There's no way that the norovirus would have cleared this quickly. Tell the others I'll see them tomorrow".

As Sandi said goodbye and put the phone down, a thought crossed her mind. The only other time that she remembered her friend and colleague taking sick leave, or being this poorly, was when she was pregnant with Danny. Francesca's pregnancy with Doug had been remarkably easy, and she'd suffered no ill effects whatsoever, working right up until two days before his birth, but with Danny it had been different. Francesca had suffered severe and crippling morning sickness, and had been extremely uncomfortable for the duration of her pregnancy, stopping working nearly two months prior to his birth because she simply couldn't cope with working in addition to running a household, looking after three children and feeling so rough.

Francesca was having similar flashbacks. She was on the pill, so in theory she shouldn't be pregnant, but as a GP she knew that the pill wasn't always completely effective, especially if you didn't always take it at the same time every day. They'd had a wonderful holiday in Thailand in October half term, the children having had an additional week this year, meaning that the family could enjoy a two week break without the feeling of guilt of taking the kids out of school, and thinking back now she knew that she had not necessarily been as meticulous as she should have about taking the preventative medication. Could she be pregnant? As a doctor, it would be the first question she would ask of a patient presenting with her symptoms, yet the thought hadn't occurred to her until now, despite feeling irritable and off colour for days, and feeling particularly queasy in the mornings for the past two weeks. Initially she'd thought that perhaps that had been her body fighting off the norovirus to which her family had succumbed, but now, she wasn't so sure.

Her mind was reeling. It wouldn't be the end of the world if she was pregnant, as after all she was very happily married, and they already had four children, so a fifth wouldn't change things that drastically, but she and Ed had agreed after Danny, and her difficult pregnancy, that they didn't want any more children and their balanced family with two sons and two daughters was enough. They also had plans that, now their youngest child was also at school full time, they could focus more on themselves and their careers. Timing wise, a pregnancy now wasn't great. With Ed about to enter this venture with Adam, they really needed for her to be working, and if she was expecting, and if she was going to suffer as much as she did when she was pregnant with Danny, then this could be a problem. As the senior partner, there was a small income regardless of whether she worked herself as a GP, and obviously she was entitled to statutory maternity leave, but the income from that was minimal compared to her salary if she worked full time.

Deciding that she needed to know one way or the other, and berating herself for leaving her medical bag at the surgery the night before in her rush to get home; forgetfulness was another symptom of pregnancy she chastised herself, Francesca ran upstairs and threw on some clothes, because pregnant or not, she was not going out in public in her nightgown and dressing gown, albeit clean ones that she'd put on having showered when she got out of bed. Blipping the lock on her BMW, and throwing her handbag onto the passenger seat, she climbed in to the driver's seat and reversed out onto the road, heading for the little parade of shops about a mile away, where she knew there was a chemist that would sell the product she needed.

Half an hour later, she was at home again, and peeing on a stick. She knew, as a medically trained professional, that whilst these tests were sometimes inaccurate with a negative result, they never gave a false positive, yet she had still purchased three different tests, all of which she hoped to do before Ed returned home that evening, because she needed to be absolutely sure. Confident, self-assured Dr Francesca Marten had been replaced, for now at least, by nervous and uncertain Mrs Ed Smithers, who seemed to have left her medical brain at work along with her bag, and right now was demonstrating what could only be considered as 'baby brain'.

The first test she completed came back positive. So did the second. Francesca knew there was no getting around it, and that she was pregnant, but she had just started the third test when she heard her father's key in the lock and the excited voices of her two sons as they tore through the hallway and into the kitchen, searching for her and for food and not necessarily in that order. Placing the stick on the windowsill behind the toilet, and not waiting the three minutes needed to see the result, Francesca tidied herself up and went downstairs to greet her family.

"I hate to say this sweetheart, but you look totally washed out" Douggie said kindly, as his daughter appeared beside him in the kitchen.

"Thanks Dad" Francesca sighed ruefully, knowing that her appearance had more to do with the shock of discovering she was expecting again, than of her illness, but not wishing to enlighten her father until she'd had the opportunity to discuss it with her husband. Both boys wrapped themselves around her waist and animatedly told her about their respective days at school, vying for her attention.

"Let your mum have a few minutes peace now lads" Douggie said, recognising that Francesca most definitely wasn't herself yet and handing them each a sandwich he'd thrown together in the short time they'd been back in the house.

"Go in the lounge and eat this and I'll come in soon" adding for Francesca's benefit "Why don't you go back to bed for a bit love, you look totally done in. I'll see to the kids. You rest".

Part of Francesca wanted to argue that actually, there was nothing wrong with her that wouldn't be put right when another baby made his or her way into their lives in a few months' time, and that she couldn't spend the duration of her pregnancy resting when her husband was about to embark on a new business. After all, the plan was that she would be the breadwinner for the next few months, but she knew that right now, she simply needed time to process everything, and to work out what she would say to Ed when he returned that evening, and therefore she gratefully accepted her father's offer and took herself back to her bedroom.

11

"Morning Jim, how was your Christmas" Dave Bradley cheerfully greeted his colleague as they walked through the huge revolving doors of reception into the big, modern glass building that housed Sphere Pharmaceuticals, the company which Jim had worked for over the past ten years, and which had relocated to Brighton just over a year previously, taking Jim and his family with them.

"Difficult" was all Jim said in response. He had, in fact, absolutely hated Christmas and felt more alone now than he had when Hannah had first passed away. Everyone said that each first was the most challenging to overcome, and his experience was certainly that to date, but Jim couldn't ever imagine a time when he'd be truly happy again.

The hardest thing he endured at the moment, was dropping the boys off at school, something he had done just half an hour earlier, as Jamie and Robbie returned to school for the new term. Jamie was in Year 2 now, and Robbie in Reception. Jim rarely travelled by car himself, having been used to walking to work when Hannah was alive, in order to allow her free use of their shared car, and therefore he didn't feel the need to use it now. The children were at a school just a couple of roads away from their home, and his office was just over a mile further along the main road, so, thanks to the fantastic breakfast club offered at Hilltop Primary School where the boys were educated, he could drop them off at eight in the morning, and still be at work on foot less than half an hour later. The only downside was that his route to work each morning took him past the scene of Hannah's fatal accident. The zebra crossing where a drunk driver had failed to stop and had sent her flying through his front windscreen and out through the rear. Attempts had been made at the scene to revive her, but it had been useless. She was taken by ambulance to their local hospital, but declared dead on arrival. Every time he walked past that crossing, his heart broke just a little bit more. He didn't think he would ever get used to walking past it without remembering the utter loss and devastation he'd felt when the police had arrived at his office asking to speak to him. Nothing could ever prepare you for that sort of news.

Breaking the news of their mother's death to the boys had been even worse. He had arrived at their school just as the children were going back into class for their afternoon lessons and had stood by the gate watching as Jamie lined up with his teacher, clearly out of breath having spent the whole of his post lunch break running around, no doubt playing football. He hadn't seen Robbie, as the nursery class operated a slightly different timetable to the rest of the school, and were kept separate at break times, but he knew that somehow he was going to have to break the news to both boys that Mummy wouldn't be coming to collect them that day, or indeed any other. Mummy would not be coming home.

It had taken every ounce of strength that he had to ring the buzzer for the school reception. He must have looked dreadful, having just come from the hospital where he'd wanted to see Hannah, but been advised against it, as her severe injuries had disfigured her once beautiful body. The receptionist was clearly wary of him, and asked him to prove his identity as she had not previously met Jim, his wife having been in charge of childcare and the school runs, but once she was satisfied that he really was Jamie and Robbie's father, and clearly distressed by his breakdown in front of her at the mention of Hannah's name, sobbing uncontrollably, she had summonsed the headteacher who had immediately ushered the younger man into his office. Jim had explained to Mr Roberts, the kindly man in his sixties who ran the Primary School, the events of the morning after Hannah had delivered their children into the care of him and his staff, and Mr Roberts then helped him to tell the boys, first Jamie and then Robbie, what had taken place. Jim shuddered as he remembered every detail of that day and those that followed. Many of his memories from the time of Hannah's death were hazy, but that day would remain etched on his heart and mind forever.

And now, here he was, back at work. Everyone was, like Dave, still full of their tales of Christmas cheer and excited for the new year ahead, but Jim felt more depressed than ever. He knew he needed to find a way to move forward with his life, rather than going through the motions of living which was what he knew he was currently doing, but he simply didn't have either the energy or the inclination to do anything different at the moment. Were Hannah able to see him now, his eyes welling up as he remembered that awful day, she'd be furious, he thought. Hannah was very much one for making the most of every second, and yet he knew there had been several missed opportunities over the past few months which he'd not even considered taking, for fear of more change disrupting the boys lives further, yet he knew that in reality, the boys were proving extremely resilient and coping remarkably well with the loss of their mother, and it was he who was scared of further disruption to the equilibrium.

The main problem, Jim realised now, was that other than his parents-in-law, Mavis and Peter, all of his family had seemed to brush off Hannah's passing as something which was literally dead and buried. His family hadn't meant to be cruel, but none of them had ever been particularly close to Hannah, despite all her best efforts to ingratiate herself in their affections, and so they weren't particularly bothered by her loss. One of their primary reasons for agreeing they should move to Brighton when the company relocated, was to be closer to his side of the family, and to build better relationships with his parents and sister, yet the reality was that as all the adults in his family worked, childcare in the school holidays had fallen predominantly to Mavis and Peter, who had alternated between having the boys stay at their house from Monday to Friday one week and staying at Jim's themselves to look after the children during his working day the next. His mum did the odd school pick up for him if he needed to work late, and he occasionally saw his parents at weekends, but he'd seen about as much of his sister as he had of his brother-in-law Adam since the funeral, and Sarah didn't have the excuse of living on another continent, as she was only a mere ten miles up the road.

Over the Christmas period, Hannah not being there had been particularly prevalent in his mind. He hadn't begrudged Mavis and Peter their trip to New York to spend Christmas with their son, and fully understood their reasons for going abroad, but despite his assurances to them that he wanted to spend Christmas with his parents this year, it was actually the last place he had wanted to be. The boys had enjoyed their day, and it was nice for them to waken on Christmas morning in their own home and see the stockings that 'Santa' had filled for them at the end of their beds, but he would have loved to have enjoyed Mavis' renowned breakfast on Christmas morning, and eaten a traditional turkey dinner at lunchtime, not to mention the massive spread she would have laid on a few hours later for tea, or the Boxing Day 'leftovers' meal which would contain even more food that he certainly hadn't seen the day before.

In contrast, his own mother had decided that cooking was too much trouble and had therefore booked them all into her local pub for lunch, but there was nothing on the menu suitable for two young children and most of the lunch guests were clearly very much the worse for alcohol which only served to remind Jim about the drunk who had killed his beloved wife. When they left the pub, only two hours after first gathering together, there seemed to be an expectation that everyone would return to their own homes, meaning he had to conjure up food for his sons who both claimed to be starved, when, in a complete parenting fail, he hadn't anticipated needing much food over Christmas. The only day he'd really enjoyed in the course of the festivities was New Year's Day which he'd spent with the boys at Mavis and Peter's house, and then the previous Saturday when Hannah's family had all made the effort to travel to Brighton to spend another day with him and the boys.

Mulling all this over in his head, Jim began to seriously question whether he was doing the right thing staying with Sphere and continuing to live in Brighton. He didn't even really enjoy his job anymore. Hearing Adam so fired up about the new challenges he would face moving back to the UK and starting up his own business had made him realise that whereas, once upon a time, he relished each new day at work, loving the challenges he faced, now he was just doing what had to be done as a means to an end, and there was certainly no passion in his work anymore. Maybe it was time to think about moving on. The kids loved their school, and they had friends there, but they had made new friends when they'd relocated from Surrey the previous year. Were they young enough and resilient enough to adapt if he uprooted them again, he wondered? Should he be making life changing decisions when he was still grieving? Was it a good idea to make big decisions on his own? There were so many questions flying around his head, but he kept coming back to the same one; what would Hannah have me do? He couldn't ask her, as she was no longer here to consult, but he was sure that he knew the answer, and a quick telephone call to her mother confirmed it.

"Follow your heart, Jim, that's all you can do. The boys will be fine, as long as they have you, and they'll always have us too. Peter and I will support you whatever you decide, but if you're not happy where you are, then it's time to make a change".

Jim had never been one to act on impulse before, but now he understood why Adam had been so enthused in the past week. There was something hugely invigorating about taking control and doing something positive. Searching on the internet for jobs in Surrey, he found one at a pharmaceutical company based in Weybridge, which was only a few miles from their old home in Leatherhead. It wasn't exactly a promotion, more of a sideways move, but it would definitely be different enough to his current job to offer him a new challenge. Deciding to take the plunge before his courage faded, he completed the online application form and then clicked 'submit'. Perhaps nothing would come of it, but as Dave peered round his office door and invited him out to lunch, something Dave often did, yet an invitation Jim usually declined, he felt more positive than he had in a very long time, and even accepted the offer of eating out.

12

Ed couldn't really concentrate at work, despite his best intentions to focus on the proposal he was putting forward to long standing clients. He'd also managed to liquidise some of the shares he had in Amazon, although he wasn't convinced that he'd obtained the best price that he could have got, because his mind was elsewhere. He was worried about his wife. He knew that the norovirus had swept through their home a few weeks earlier, and that unlike the rest of the family Francesca hadn't succumbed, so it was likely that she was just suffering a little later than the rest of them, but he couldn't help but be concerned because Francesca was literally never ill. This was something that never ceased to amaze him about his beloved wife; her ability to fend off all the various strains of illness which she encountered, and indeed treated others for, on a daily basis.

As soon as it was viable, he'd left the office and caught the train back to Hampton, where he'd left the car at the station, having dropped the children at school that morning. He arrived home to find all four of his children sat around the dining table, each doing their own homework under the patient guidance of their grandfather. He greeted each one in turn and then, surprised to learn that Francesca was still in bed, having received a text from her earlier that day to say that she was feeling much better, no doubt in an attempt to stop him worrying he now realised, he headed up to their room.

Francesca was curled up under the covers sleeping peacefully. Not wishing to disturb her, he quietly grabbed a pair of jeans and a casual sweater from their walk in closet, then headed into the en suite bathroom to get changed. It was then that he saw it, sat on the windowsill behind the toilet. The realisation hit him like a brick between the eyes. Suddenly everything made sense. Francesca's unusual irritation over the past few days, the being sick when she was never poorly, her complaints about putting on weight over Christmas despite seemingly not having over-indulged. She was pregnant. He should have realised sooner, but then he didn't think it was possible for her to get pregnant when they were using birth control. Maybe she had stopped taking it and not told him? No, Francesca wouldn't do that…. Would she? Did she know she was pregnant? Well, of course, she'd done a test so she must have, but when did she find out? Why had she not told him? Did she want him to find the test or was he not meant to see this? He was home early after all. His mind was reeling. At any other time, he'd be thrilled to welcome another child into their family, but he was about to enter into a life changing business venture which would leave them financially less stable for the foreseeable future. It wouldn't matter if Francesca continued earning, but a baby would change that. Was that why she had been so worried about the business idea, he wondered? Maybe she had known, albeit subconsciously, and that was why she had been so reluctant to engage with the idea.

Eventually pulling himself together enough to get changed out of his suit and into more comfortable clothing, Ed padded quietly back into their bedroom. He didn't really want to wake her from her sleep, as he knew she'd had several broken and restless nights recently, and if she was pregnant then she needed all the rest she could get, but he needed to talk to her. He couldn't just go downstairs and pretend to the family that everything was normal when it was clearly anything but. Perching on the bed beside her, he stroked the hair from her forehead off her face.

Slowly Francesca opened her eyes and blinked up at her husband. "You're home, what time is it?" she whispered, her voice hoarse from having only just woken.

"It's six o'clock" Ed replied, offering her a glass of water and helping her sit up in bed, "and it's definitely time we talked" he continued.

Francesca looked at him quizzically, and then remembered her predicament and realisation dawned. "The pregnancy test. You found the one I left in the bathroom when Dad came in with the boys?" she asked, following up with another question. "I take it that was positive too?". Ed nodded, as Francesca felt the need to explain.

"It was a comment Sandi made about me never being poorly" Francesca started. "It got me thinking that the only time I've ever felt this rough was when we were expecting Danny. I didn't think I could be pregnant because I've been on the pill, but my cycle must have got out of whack when we were in Thailand and I didn't realise. I bought three test kits, all different brands, and did them today. There's two positive ones in the bathroom bin and I was in the middle of taking a third for confirmation when I heard Dad come in. He said I looked really rough, probably the shock of discovering that I'm expecting again at my age, and suggested I come up and lie down. I completely forgot about the test I'd left on the windowsill and I was so exhausted that I literally fell asleep as soon as my head hit the pillow. Are you mad at me?".

Ed shook his head and enveloped her into a tight hug. "Not mad, it's as much my fault as yours if you're up the duff after all" he smiled "But this does kind of change things, doesn't it?".

Francesca didn't know what to say. She wanted to reassure him that nothing needed to change, but that simply wasn't true and they both knew it. No matter how established you are as parents, and no matter how secure you are financially, a new baby means a huge upheaval for the whole family, and they needed to face up to the reality.

One thing Francesca had decided though, was that this shouldn't stop Ed from going into business with Adam. Ironically, she felt more convinced than ever that Ed should take the opportunity in front of him, even though they were now potentially in a very different position financially and the risk was therefore more prevalent.

"Our lives will be turned upside down yet again by this little one" she started, wanting to convey the thoughts that had been swirling round in her head all afternoon to her husband, "but I don't want our new son or daughter to be born to a bored and grumpy Daddy" Ed looked at her somewhat indignantly as she hurriedly continued, realising that she wasn't putting this quite as well as she had hoped.

"I want you to press on with the business plan that you and Adam have and to make Smithers, Baynes and Co. the biggest and most successful consultancy firm in London" she said. "You wanted to build a company for the future of our kids, and now we're adding one more little one into the mix, but as you said yourself, we have the house as our security, we have my income, even though I'll need to take some maternity leave, and whilst we don't want to touch the money we've saved and put in trust for the kids, if we're desperate, we can dip into that for a short while, just until you and I are back to earning what we're used to".

Ed marvelled at his wife. When he'd first broached the idea of starting a business with Adam, it was fair to say she'd been much less than enthusiastic, yet here she was encouraging him to go for it when circumstances meant that it was more difficult than ever for him to do so.

Voicing his concerns that the long hours he would need to put in to get the business up and running would take him out of the home at a time when she needed him there most, and that tightening their belts financially at a time when most families found themselves spending far more than usual, no longer made this quite such a sound proposition, anyone listening would have been forgiven for thinking that Ed was trying to talk both himself and his wife out of the idea of the new business, but Francesca wouldn't let him dwell on the negatives.

"On Sunday you and Adam assured me that by the summer, you would be earning a living, albeit a modest one, from this new company. Has that prediction changed?" she asked.

"Well, no, there's no reason why we shouldn't be fully functioning and starting to turn a small profit by July" Ed replied.

"Well then," Francesca continued, "I don't know exactly when this little one was conceived, or when we will get to meet our fifth child, but I do know it's not likely to be within the next six months, so hopefully by the time he or she puts in an appearance, you'll be able to step back a little, and enjoy some paternity leave. After all, Adam and Maddie plan on spending three weeks in Florida with their families over the summer, so surely you'll be entitled to the same amount of leave with us, and let's face it; we won't be going abroad while I'm pregnant or in the first few weeks of sproglet's life so you won't be needing time off for a holiday!". Ed laughed. Francesca never ceased to amaze him with her positive outlook and her ability to make the best of every situation.

"So, when do we tell people?" he asked, gently rubbing his wife's stomach, clearly excited at the prospect of becoming a father again, now that the shock had worn off slightly.

"I'm not sure." Francesca replied. "Part of me would love to tell everyone now, to explain why I've been ill today, but I'm also worried. This baby was conceived whilst I was on the pill, which shouldn't have done any damage, but I want to be sure. I'm in my late forties now, and that's also a concern because there are other complications in pregnancy the older you get. I think we should be sure of a due date too, before we tell anyone else. I'll organise a scan when I'm at work tomorrow, and then we can make a more informed decision as to what happens next. Is that okay?".

Ed looked lovingly into her eyes as he said "You're the medical expert, and in all things kids, you're the boss. You just tell me where I need to be when for the scan and I'll be there. We're in this together. Okay?".

Francesca smiled, kissed Ed on the lips and gently whispered "Okay". For the first time in weeks, she felt truly happy. This might not be a planned pregnancy, but the baby would be loved, there was no doubt about that.

13

Arriving at the departure terminal at Heathrow Airport for the second time in less than three weeks, Maddie marvelled at how much her life had transformed in such an incredibly short space of time. Three weeks earlier, Maddie had been personal assistant to the director of Houlton Hotels, and had been excited about her forthcoming trip to New York, where she planned to spend her Christmas break, having been unceremoniously ditched for the holiday season by her much loved siblings, who had all chosen to spend Christmas with their respective in-laws, effectively rendering her alone. Annoyed with her family for their lack of compassion, and for changing lifetime traditions of being together for Christmas Day, regardless of other people, as a result of her father's passing earlier in 2019, Maddie had travelled alone to the airport straight after work on the Friday before Christmas, anticipating a magical break in her favourite city, but without any concept of the life changes which were about to befall her. Now, here she was at the same airport on the Wednesday two and a half weeks later, with the man she had met and fallen in love with during her brief stay in New York, stood beside her, saying goodbye to her sister who had driven them to the airport.

"Have an amazing time" gushed Juliet, adding "I'm so jealous that you're going back again Mads. I'd love to go to New York and here you are going back for the second time in as many weeks". Maddie hugged her sister tightly and explained for the umpteenth time that this trip was not a holiday, but would involve lots of work. She thought that if she said it often enough, she might actually start to believe it herself. Adam was clear about all they needed to accomplish whilst in the city, but she couldn't help but feel that her presence would be more ornamental than useful. Neither she nor Adam wanted to be apart from the other, but in reality she didn't believe there was a tremendous amount she could realistically do, as whilst he was happy to give her autonomy over staging his apartment, only he could decide whether that would be for sale or rental, and only he would have the authority to act on decisions made. She could offer some assistance, but envisaged most of her planned ten days in New York being spent cooking, cleaning and generally behaving like a housewife, rather than being of use to him in the true sense of a personal assistant.

"I'll be here to collect you at 9am on the eighteenth" said Juliet, reluctantly letting go of her sister, adding "Look after her Adam" to the man stood beside them, as she briefly kissed him on the cheek.

"I will, Juliet" he assured the younger woman, to which he received a rather indignant look from Maddie who told both of them that she certainly didn't need looking after.

Maddie was becoming alarmingly accustomed to travelling in style she realised, as they scooted past the majority of the crowds and into the upper-class lounge. She had suggested to Adam that perhaps it would be more frugal, given their current position, to fly in economy, but he wouldn't hear of it. He also seemed very comfortable taking advantage of all the perks that upper class offered, including the complimentary champagne upon boarding, but Maddie preferred to stick with coffee. Soon, they were settled in their luxurious seats, and flying over the Atlantic, destined for America.

It was early evening when they reached what Maddie thought would be their final destination for the day; Adam's luxurious penthouse apartment in Tribeca, one of the trendiest and most expensive parts of Manhattan. Although it was only around four in the afternoon in New York, and despite snoozing her bed on the plane, Maddie was exhausted because the previous day had been a manic rush to make all the necessary preparations for leaving the country again at such short notice, and it was, after all, the equivalent of 9pm at home. Adam, however, had other ideas. He had little in the way of groceries in his apartment, having cleared out the fresh food before returning to the UK on New Year's Eve, not knowing when he would eventually return to his penthouse, and he was not adept at keeping supplies in the freezer for situations like this, which is what Maddie would have done had it been her; indeed stocking the freezer had been one of her tasks the previous day. Adam wanted to take them out for dinner somewhere fancy, suggesting that they freshen up and then head to midtown, but Maddie simply didn't have the energy and suggested that instead they should visit the 24 hour deli on the corner of his street to buy a few essentials and that she would rustle them up something in his high tech kitchen so that they could then get an early night.

Once their shopping mission was complete, and their suitcases deposited in Adam's bedroom, Maddie took the opportunity to look around his now familiar apartment. The view over the Hudson from his lounge window was as spectacular as ever, but the penthouse seemed to have lost its personal touch since she was last there. Mildly offended that the items they had purchased to prepare for his parents' arrival two weeks earlier seemed to have disappeared, she challenged Adam as to why his apartment once again appeared unloved and unlived in. Adam was quick to explain that on the day he'd made the decision to return to the UK he had begun the process of packing every personal possession that he owned, including the rug that they'd bought for the lounge, the artwork which she had gifted him for Christmas and all of the other homely touches that they had bought together, intending to try and get them back to England. Had his Dad not intervened and suggested that perhaps for now, he should just focus on taking one suitcase full of clothes which he would require whilst he was away, every possession would have travelled across the ocean at outlandish additional baggage costs. He hadn't, however, bothered to unpack those other cases and boxes, simply stashing them in a cupboard instead, as he didn't intend to be living in the apartment long enough to care about its appearance in future.

Maddie was relieved that he hadn't simply removed all traces of her from the apartment, and promised to unpack for him the following day. Adam was about to object when she reminded him that the whole idea was to stage his apartment so that it would appeal to potential buyers or renters, and therefore transforming it back into a home was important.

"You're right, sorry, I didn't think of it like that" Adam said. "I'll show you where I've stashed it all".

Once satisfied that she could easily and quickly return the apartment to the state in which she'd left it two weeks previously, Maddie set about making them something to eat. Neither of them was particularly hungry, as they'd eaten plenty on the plane, but they knew that sustenance was important if they were to stand a hope of staying awake and combating the impending threat of jet lag.

The following morning, Adam headed out to the office at 7am, leaving Maddie pottering in the kitchen. They had decided the previous evening that, due to the lack of supplies in the apartment and the fact that they would both be there for at least the next ten days, there was a real need for some food in the apartment. Maddie intended to travel home in time for a planned outing with friends to the theatre. Adam couldn't yet say when he would be ready to depart, but whether he joined Maddie on her return flight home or not, they both needed to eat in the meantime.

Walking through the familiar streets to the hypermarket, Maddie felt different somehow to the way she had on previous visits to the city. She no longer felt like a fully-fledged tourist, but more like a resident. Okay, so she wasn't going to be living there for long, but unlike on her last visit, and those that preceded it, she didn't feel the urgent need to take in every sight, participate in every tourist activity and view every landmark. In contrast, she was happy to power walk through the streets to her destination, barely looking up at her surroundings, and jostle with the other residents in the supermarket to ensure that she bought the best possible produce, just as she would have done in her local Tesco or Sainsburys at home.

Once confident that she had enough supplies to ensure that they could eat comfortably for the near future without the need to travel far from the apartment, she returned to what she still considered to be Adam's home, even though he seemed to have mentally disentangled himself from it already. Starting in the kitchen, she began the process of making the place look and feel more homely again. She cooked a casserole, which filled the apartment with aromas of lamb and vegetables, thinking that having something filling, warming and nutritious for their evening meal would be good, then she began to unpack all of the personal touches which she'd introduced on her last visit. First she found the comfy scatter cushions which she had suggested Adam buy to take the stark edges off the large black leather sofas, then she rolled out the gorgeous matching teal rug which made the lounge far more comfortable under foot and added much needed colour to the monochrome colour scheme. Finally she found the carefully wrapped art work which she had brought for Adam from a street artist in Times Square, depicting the city skyline lit up at night, in hues of blue, green and purple, with a helicopter flying past, and hung it back where he had placed it upon opening it on Christmas Day.

Confident that the lounge was now more welcoming, she set to work in the other rooms. She had brought a beautiful plum coloured bedding set from home for the bedroom she and Adam were sharing, which brightened up the room significantly, and breaking the habit of a lifetime, she decided to actually unpack her suitcase, feeling that the presence of her clothes in the closet and her trinkets on the sleek dressing table would make the bedroom looked more lived in. Deciding that more accessories were needed to truly stage the apartment as a home, Maddie then headed out on a mission. She had been told that Bed, Bath and Beyond was a great place to buy beautiful home accessories, so checked on line for the nearest store to Tribeca, and headed out in the direction of the Flatiron building, determined to purchase a number of items which would serve to transform the monochrome palace into a welcoming and cosy home.

14

Francesca's morning sickness abated slightly over the course of the week, but she felt rougher than ever when she and Ed headed to the local hospital for their first scan. They were booked in at ten in the morning, and then due to see a friend of Francesca's who specialised in obstetrics and gynaecology afterwards for a general health check. It took every ounce of strength that she had to get in the car that Friday morning and not to vomit all over the seats of Ed's precious Audi SUV. Ed had taken the day off work, and indeed had worked from home more than in the office all week, wanting to support his wife and help with caring for the brood they already had, and he was now driving them to the hospital for their appointments.

Neither of them quite understood their nervousness as Ed parked the car in the large and busy car park. It wasn't as if they'd not been through this before. Both of their sons had been born in this hospital, and they had been here for the twelve, and twenty, week scans for each child, plus some additional scans when Francesca had been expecting Danny because she'd been so poorly throughout that pregnancy that they had been deemed necessary. It was silly therefore to be so worried, Francesca chastised herself, yet she somehow couldn't help it and neither, it would appear, could Ed.

Taking hold of his wife's hand and leading her up the steps to the prenatal unit of the hospital, Ed felt like his stomach was in knots. Like Francesca, he had an uneasy feeling which he couldn't quite explain, and whilst both of them were trying not to show it, neither was very good at hiding feelings from the other after ten years of marriage, and as many more years again, together as a couple.

"Here we are then" Ed tried to sound positive and upbeat as they entered the reception area. "This is one place I didn't think we'd be visiting again". Francesca smiled a wry smile, then gave her name and details to the receptionist.

The sonographer who was due to scan Francesca was running late, so the couple had an agonising wait in the bright, artificially lit reception area before they were finally called through into a little room. Ed clutched Francesca's hand tightly as she lay on the bed, eyes glued to the screen even before the scan had even begun.

"Relax Mrs Smithers" the sonographer instructed. "It's not good for little one if you're so stressed".

Francesca wanted to scream "I know, I'm a bloody doctor" at the young girl, who couldn't have been qualified for more than about five minutes, as she didn't look any older than Bronwyn, but decided against it. There was, after all, a reason why she used her married name when she was receiving medical treatment, as everyone knows that doctors make terrible patients, and there was no need for anyone in the radiology department to know that her usual identity was Dr Marten. Instead, she loosened her grip on Ed's hand and took some deep breaths.

Francesca and Ed's attempts at relaxing didn't last long. The sonographer, clearly inexperienced, located a heartbeat with minimal difficulty, although it sounded a little unusual to Ed's untrained ears, but then seemed to have incredible trouble examining the foetus.

"I'm really sorry" she said, removing the doppler from Francesca's stomach almost as soon as she'd started, "but I'm going to have to ask my colleague to come in. Please just bear with me for a few moments".

Immediately, Francesca and Ed's stress levels went through the roof. "What's wrong with our baby?" Ed asked, half directing the question at the young girl conducting the scan and half at his wife, as obviously he knew of her medical training, even if the sonographer didn't. The young girl simply offered platitudes that everything was fine and that the baby was just proving a little awkward, so required a more experienced sonographer, as she scuttled out of the room as quickly as humanly possible. Francesca remained silent, internally wishing that she'd grabbed hold of the doppler herself and continued to conduct the scan without the aid of the supposedly trained professional beside her, but knowing that this would have been considered inappropriate, she had chosen to remain lying motionless on the bed.

Left alone in the room, Ed looked pleadingly at Francesca for answers, but his wife was unable to give any reassurance. "I didn't really see anything. She stopped the scan before I'd had chance to get a proper look".

Their original sonographer returned to the room a few minutes later, with a much older lady in tow. The new sonographer, whom Francesca recognised from previous visits both as a patient and as a doctor, took her position at the ultrasound machine, whilst the younger girl sat to one side.

"I'm so sorry Mrs Smithers, Mr Smithers" began the lady then looking at Francesca properly for the first time "Oh, Doctor Marten, I didn't realise it was you. Lovely to see you again". The young sonographer baulked behind her colleague, recognising that this lady she had attempted to scan unsuccessfully was actually a medical professional, and shifted to one side, allowing her superior better access.

"Hello Betty" Francesca managed meekly. "I'm sorry to be such a pain". The older lady laughed off the apology, stating firmly that there was nothing to be sorry about and that she'd soon get them back on track.

Nothing could have prepared Ed and Francesca for the news they were about to receive. One unplanned and unexpected baby had been enough of a shock, but when Betty resumed the scan, she quickly found that there was not only one baby growing inside Francesca's uterus, but two. They were going to become parents to twins. Not only that, but the pregnancy was much further advanced than either of them had anticipated, and Betty suspected that Francesca was approximately four months pregnant, meaning that the babies had been conceived in early September, not late October as Francesca had believed. She predicted the babies' due date to be around 5th June, but warned that as the babies were twins, and as Francesca was considered to be an older mother now, she would probably be advised to have an elective caesarean section at thirty seven to thirty eight weeks gestation, meaning that she would be booked in for this around the end of May. The good news, however, was that both babies seemed to be growing well, and that although Francesca wasn't showing in the traditional sense, the fact that she'd never really lost her baby weight after her previous pregnancies meant that there was plenty of room for the babies to grow.

Finally regaining his composure enough to ask, Ed voiced his desire to know the gender of the babies. Francesca informed him that at least one of them was a girl, a fact Betty was happy to confirm, but as the other twin was hiding behind his or her sibling, it was more difficult to ascertain the second child's gender.

"Wow, a daughter. I didn't think we made those ourselves" he said incredulously, referring to the fact that their previous two pregnancies had resulted in sons.

"No, but at least we have experience in bringing them up" Francesca countered, explaining to the puzzled sonographers that they had two adoptive daughters and two natural born sons.

"Well now it looks like you'll be adding two more little humans to that merry band of children you already have" Betty said kindly, "and at least one of those will be another daughter. Who knows, you might end up with one of each. That would really balance out your family".

Ed had so many questions as they sat back down in the waiting room before being called in to see the obstetrics specialist, yet he didn't dare voice any of them for fear of upsetting Francesca. She had already explained to him that sometimes the contraceptive pill simply wasn't completely effective, and that changes in circumstance could result in unplanned pregnancies, citing their vacation in Thailand and the changes in time zone and food as the most likely culprit, which made sense when they were potentially talking about a late October conception, but he couldn't help but wonder how this particular pregnancy, with twins no less, had gone undetected for four months? He knew that the pill meant she didn't have periods anymore, but surely, she should have, and would have, recognised the changes in her body as the babies began to grow inside of her? Come to that, how had he not seen any signs previously? He knew her body as well as he knew his own, and yet he hadn't noticed. How was that possible?

Continuing this thought process, he remembered Betty's declaration that these babies must have been conceived in early September. If that was correct, he couldn't quite get his head round what changes had occurred in their routine which might have led to a disruption in Francesca's taking of the pill. A beach holiday in Corfu in August was a lovely break from the daily grind, but surely not the sort of departure from reality which would have prevented the contraption from working? Ed also desperately wanted to ask whether or not their babies would have been adversely affected by her continued taking of the contraceptive medication throughout the first four months of the pregnancy, but again he didn't dare do so, because he didn't want her to think that he was in any way accusing of her of harming them.

Dr Martha Andrews, a good friend of Francesca's from medical school, was blunt and direct in her approach and this came as a relief to Ed. Without him needing to ask, she managed to answer most of the questions which were swimming around in his brain. Dr Andrews began by reassuring them that it was highly unlikely that either baby had been harmed in any way by Francesca continuing to take the pill after conception, as the most likely side effect of this would have been an ectopic pregnancy, which the scan had already confirmed was not a concern. The fact that the babies had made it to four months gestation, without any adverse side effects showing themselves, was also a very good sign. Francesca's age would likely have masked the pregnancy, as she put the subtle changes in her body down to the potential onset of the menopause, and having never really regained her previously slim figure after Danny's birth, and with the twins resting quite close to her spine, her bump was not yet truly noticeable and the twins would only just have started moving around, which is probably what had brought on the nausea she was now experiencing.

As Betty had predicted, Dr Andrews recommended that Francesca be booked in for an elective caesarean section delivery on or around the 20th May, as she didn't feel it was sensible medically for either Francesca or her babies to take the pregnancy beyond that, or to risk a natural birth, particularly considering the fact that Francesca was now in her mid-forties and that the babies had been conceived unconventionally. This led Francesca to query why she might have conceived in September, explaining to her friend that there had not been any particular disruption to their routine at that time, and therefore she couldn't explain it. Knowing that the family liked to travel, Dr Andrews asked Francesca whether she had received any immunisations around that time, and suddenly the penny dropped. At the end of the school summer holidays, the entire family had been vaccinated against malaria in preparation for their planned visit to Thailand later in the year. Francesca mentally kicked herself, knowing that the advice following any form of vaccination was to use additional forms of contraception for two or three weeks post immunisation, yet at the time it simply hadn't occurred to her, and of course her colleague who administered the injection wouldn't have lectured her like he would other patients, as she was his boss and should know that without being reminded!

"It just goes to prove that we doctors really are poor patients" she said, as she finished explaining her lightbulb moment to Ed and Martha, adding "I'm so sorry Ed, it's completely my fault that we're in this mess".

Ed was quick to reassure his wife. They certainly hadn't planned on having another baby, much less two more children, yet he was actually quite excited now that he was getting used to the idea, especially knowing that they were going to have at least one baby daughter, something neither of them had previously experienced, and he certainly didn't want Francesca to feel the burden of blame.

"It's as much my fault as yours, sweetheart. You didn't make these babies on your own, so I think I need to shoulder some of the responsibility too" he smiled lovingly at his wife. "It's not like we don't have a wonderful, loving and welcoming home for them to be born into is it? They're going to have two big sisters and two big brothers who will love them just as much as their mummy and daddy, not to mention all their other relatives. This is not a mess, just a new challenge. We can do this. 2020 is going to be all about new beginnings."

Francesca was grateful to Ed for his undying support, despite still feeling guilty that they were in this predicament now, at a time when Ed should really be focusing on his work, but she was also beginning to come around to the idea, and when Ed put it like that, how could she argue? They would welcome these babies into their family, just as she had welcomed each of their other children in various circumstances, and they would love them unconditionally, because that was what being a good parent was all about. As for everything else she was worried about; money, work, childcare. Those things were just details, and they'd figure them out later as a family.

15

Jim couldn't quite believe his eyes when he'd logged in to his email two nights' previously. He'd been offered an interview with the pharmaceutical company that he'd applied to on a whim. Claxton Pharmaceutical had taken him seriously and actually wanted to see him. The interview was scheduled for 9.30am on the Friday morning, which involved quite a logistical challenge. He dropped the boys off with a neighbour, who had children at the same school, just after 7am, thanking her for the umpteenth time for agreeing to help him out, then battled with the traffic on the A23, M23 and M25 to get to Weybridge on time. Driving at that time of the morning, and in those sort of rush hour conditions on some of the country's busiest motorways was not easy, and certainly not something he enjoyed, but mercifully he pulled into the car park at Claxton Pharmaceuticals at 9.15am, meaning he'd arrived with fifteen minutes to spare, despite the horrendous traffic that he'd encountered on route.

It had been a long time since Jim was required to wear a full suit for work, as Sphere had a relaxed dress code which meant that his usual attire was a pair of chinos and an open collar, button down shirt. The only suit he owned was the one which he'd bought for Hannah's funeral, and he didn't feel entirely comfortable wearing that today, yet he'd not had enough notice of the interview to have time to borrow or buy anything different.

"That's what happens when you do things impulsively" he'd chastised himself, as he got dressed that morning, donning a bright blue shirt and silver tie which cheered up the stark black suit somewhat, and mentally promising himself that he'd go suit shopping at the weekend, because whether or not he was successful in the interview today, he would need suits in future; either for more interviews, or for this job, if by some miracle he actually managed to secure it.

Claxton Pharmaceuticals was situated in the middle of a large trading estate, just outside the town of Weybridge, close to the old Brooklands race track, remnants of which could be seen from the road as he'd driven in, religiously following the satellite navigation lady's instructions and hoping that she wasn't taking him on a wild goose chase as she uttered "in one hundred feet, turn left. In fifty feet, turn right. In eighty feet, bear left at the fork" and so on. Walking into the reception area of the large concrete building, which from the outside looked more like a warehouse than an office building, he could have been forgiven for wondering if he was in the right place, but the signage all assured him that he was, indeed, at his intended destination, and when he gave his name to the clerk on reception she ticked him off on what seemed like an incredibly long list of potential candidates and asked him to take a seat on one of the tub chairs to his left.

Mark Edwards, the lead interviewer, and the only person on the panel whose name Jim remembered, was a man in his early fifties, Jim guessed, and well over six foot tall, so towered over Jim as he stood to greet him. The other panellists were a lady roughly the same age as Jim, dressed in what could only be described as a power suit and killer heels, and a man who didn't look old enough to have left school, let alone be on an interview panel, dressed in a sharp silver grey suit with a white shirt, pink tie and unbelievably shiny shoes. Jim felt his insides turn to jelly as he greeted each one and silently wondered what on earth had made him decide that putting himself through this torture was actually a good idea.

The questions the panel asked of him were all relatively easy for a man of Jim's experience to answer, and if anything he began to wonder whether he might be overqualified for the job, but then when Mark outlined the roles and responsibilities he would have, he understood why they were looking for someone well qualified. If successful, Jim's role would be to visit all the different doctors in the South East region of England, explaining the products offered by Claxton and answering queries that the medical professionals may have, in an attempt to convince them to prescribe those medications to their patients. This would require building strong working relationships with practice managers and GPs in local surgeries, as well as administrative managers and medical staff in hospitals. He would need a full working knowledge of every medication Claxton produced, as well as significant knowledge of other rival products, and he would need to be a confident salesman.

In terms of the knowledge, Jim had a very clear understanding of the different types of medication Claxton produced, as they were one of Sphere's main rivals. He currently worked on Sphere's marketing team and therefore knew the benefits and disadvantages of the different brands inside out, but convincing medical practitioners to prescribe the Claxton products over other brands would be a new challenge. It would also mean driving around the county, something Jim was also unaccustomed to, as he walked most places, but he had a clean driving licence and it would get him out and meeting people again, which somehow appealed. He would also get a company vehicle, which would be replaced every three years, meaning that he wouldn't have the worry of whether his car would pass its MOT and other road safety requirements each year, as it was getting quite old now.

Finally leaving Claxton just after midday, having been given a tour of the offices and a brief history of the company by the young man in shiny shoes, who, it transpired, was a very junior employee who was being given the opportunity to sit in on the interviews for experience, but not part of the decision making team, Jim made his way back to the Marks and Spencer's that he'd seen on his way into the Brooklands estate. Initially his intention was to grab a quick coffee, before popping in to see his parents-in-law on his way home, but acting on impulse once again, he started shopping and by the time he returned to his car, he had three new suits, four new shirts and two new ties. His bank balance was also significantly lighter.

Mavis and Peter were, as always, thrilled to see their son-in-law and made him very welcome at their lunch table, even though he'd not warned them of his arrival until he'd left the Brooklands shopping centre less than half an hour previously. He hadn't been certain that he would have the time to visit, and not wanting to make promises which he couldn't follow through, had said nothing about his interview until he arrived on their doorstep. Explaining his attire, and his decision to apply for jobs back in Surrey, he was greeted with total support from Mavis and Peter, who assured him that they would do everything they could to support him, including offering him and the children a home in the interim period, should he need to start work sooner than selling his existing home and buying a new house would allow.

Feeling remarkably positive, and full of anticipation for the future, Jim had headed back down to Brighton, arriving well before the end of after school club to collect his children. His early arrival on a Friday was not that unusual, as he often worked flexi-time during the week, skipping lunch breaks so as to leave an hour early on a Friday afternoon to start the weekend with his sons as soon as possible, but the staff running the programme noticed the significant change in his dress code, and commented that they had never seen him in a suit. He hadn't wanted to say anything about potentially relocating in front of the boys, as he'd yet to tell them the purpose of his early start and change in routine that morning, so simply said, as he had to his children, that he'd been dressed for an important meeting at work and left it at that.

They had just walked in through the door at home, when Jim's mobile telephone buzzed in his pocket. He was tempted to ignore it, as he wanted to make the most of the additional time with his children, but something told him that he needed to take the call.

"Jim McDonald" he said, introducing himself in greeting as he answered the telephone.

"Good afternoon Mr McDonald, this is Mark Edwards from Claxton Pharmaceuticals. We met this morning". Jim wasn't entirely sure what to say. All correspondence prior to the interview had been conducted via email and he had therefore not expected a telephone call of any kind, but knew he had to be professional.

"Good afternoon Mr Edwards. How lovely to speak to you again". As he said the words, he realised how cheesy they sounded, almost crawling, yet he couldn't rewind the conversation and start again, so he waited with bated breath for the other man to speak.

After what seemed like an age, although in reality it was little more than two or three seconds, Mark Edwards spoke again. "My colleague Rebecca and I were extremely impressed with the interview which you gave this morning. We would like to invite you for a follow up session on Tuesday of next week, which will be a whole day process, involving a series of workshops and tasks. Would you be willing to attend?".

Jim couldn't really say no, as he too had been impressed by what he had seen that morning, and could see himself working at Claxton, but he knew that logistically a whole day in Weybridge was going to be a challenge, not least from a childcare point of view, let alone completing whatever workshop tasks were to be expected of him. Deciding that he would worry about those aspects later, he accepted the offer and said that yes, he would be willing to attend and made a note of the details, which Mark promised to put in a follow up email.

All of a sudden, his whim was turning into a real possibility, and this both excited him and scared him, but he knew that he had to give this his best shot. Thanking Mark for the opportunity, and ending the call, he quickly telephoned Mavis and explained the conversation to her. Without any further prompting, she immediately volunteered that she and Peter would come down on the Monday evening and stay the night Monday and Tuesday, meaning that childcare was taken care of. Now all Jim had to do, was explain himself at work. He had taken the day that day as holiday, but he knew that now that he potentially stood a chance of securing this new post, he really needed to admit to his employers and colleagues, that he was looking at options elsewhere. That was a conversation for Monday morning rather than now, however, and right at this moment, his priority needed to be spending quality time with his children, distracting himself from the unwelcome prospect of having to explain his position to those with whom he currently worked.

16

As she tapped away at the Mac in the loungeroom of Adam's swish apartment in New York, Maddie felt as if she were finally doing something useful. There were three estate agents, or realtors as they were known in America, coming to view the penthouse later that afternoon; a man called Russell Harris from Hobbs, Harris and Golden Realtors, a lady called Helen Schwarz from a company called Schwarz Real Estate and a JJ Lawrence from the little local Tribeca Estates firm which was based just around the corner from the apartment building. Knowing that if American realtors were anything like British Estate Agents, each would come armed with their own agenda and ideas, Maddie wanted to be fully prepared. She was therefore conducting her own brand of market research, looking for sales and rental prices for similar properties both in Tribeca, and in other upmarket parts of Manhattan.

Searching through the various properties for sale online, Maddie was shocked to discover that properties the same ilk as Adam's in Tribeca and other similar parts of Manhattan, retailed at anywhere between five and fifteen million US dollars. She was stunned. Obviously, she'd worked out by now that he was wealthy, and that he earned a significant wage from his high-powered job, but hadn't he said that he owned the apartment outright? If that were true, and even if it sold at a price somewhere in the lower end of that price bracket, that still made Adam a multi-millionaire. Surely, she would have known if that were true? She'd expected that the property would fetch somewhere in the region of half a million pounds sterling, but never imagined it was worth anything like the prices she was seeing online. Her own little house in Walton on Thames had been purchased for two hundred and fifty thousand pounds about ten years previously, and that was with the aid of a mortgage. She had seen luxury flats like Adam's for sale, but even in trendy places in London like Canary Wharf and South Kensington, she didn't anticipate them fetching more than a million pounds, and whilst a quick google search confirmed that the prices in London were significantly lower, she realised that she was possibly underestimating the property value slightly, as you'd need at least a million pounds to buy the property Adam planned on renting in Canary Wharf and double that to get anything similar in certain other parts of London.

Maddie picked her jaw up from the floor, where it had metaphorically landed in shock at the prices displayed in front of her, and suddenly felt very pleased that she'd had the foresight to do her research prior to the first agent visiting the property at midday. She wouldn't want to jeopardise Adam's chances of selling or renting because the agent saw her disbelieving face when he or she began quoting figures, thinking that perhaps Maddie had no right to be brokering the property for potential sale, not having any idea of it's true worth. Continuing with her internet search, she decided to look up rental prices. She knew that Adam had agreed to rent the property in London for £900 per calendar month, the same amount as she currently spent on her mortgage, which now seemed like small change in the grand scheme of things, and she completely understood why he was not in the least bit afraid of signing a six month lease at that price, because clearly he could well afford it. It appeared that the rental income from a property like the one in which she was currently sitting, would be around fifteen thousand dollars per month. That converted to over eleven thousand pounds sterling per month. One month's rent from this apartment would more than cover a year's lease on the flat in Canary Wharf. The figures absolutely astounded her.

Resolving to confront Adam about his wealth later, wanting to know why he had kept the extent of his fortune from her, Maddie concluded her search and set to work in the kitchen. Nothing appealed more than the smell of freshly baked cakes, so she planned on baking for the remainder of the morning, so that not only could she offer the various agents a sweet treat when they came to value the apartment, but also it would smell divine too.

Maddie had never previously received visitors into the penthouse, having always entered with Adam and the only visitors having been his parents, who like her had been given the private code for the elevator, meaning no announcement of their arrival was necessary. Hearing a strange buzzing sound coming from the handset on the coffee table in the lounge, which she had previously assumed was some form of remote control, she investigated and discovered that it was actually a type of entry phone. Speaking to Joseph, the doorman whom she had come to know quite well after all her various trips out to the shops, she discovered that her first realtor, Mr Harris, had arrived and was requesting permission to enter the elevator.

"Oh, yes, of course Joe, please let him in" she said into the device.

"Okay Ma'am, he'll be with you shortly" came the response in his strong American twang.

The elevator opened into the large lounge area of Adam's three bedroom apartment to reveal a very prim looking gentleman in a sharp navy blue suit, with matching tie and crisp white shirt, a long navy overcoat slung over the same forearm which held a smart charcoal leather briefcase.

"Good afternoon Mrs Baynes" began the man, in the most drooling of voices, holding out his right hand to shake hers firmly "Russell Harris from Hobbs, Harris and Golden at your service".

Maddie considered allowing him to continue to believe she were Adam's wife, feeling a warm tingle that she had not expected at the thought of playing the role, but decided honesty was the best policy and therefore replied "Pleased to meet you Mr Harris. Madeline Lane. I'm Mr Baynes' personal assistant". As she uttered the words, the man's demeanour immediately changed. He released her hand as if it were a piece of dirt he needed to shake off, and went from treating her as though she were the most precious jewel in the world that needed to be given the highest respect, to displaying nothing short of disdain towards her.

"Ah, well, in that case, perhaps we should just get on with viewing the apartment. I'm sure you have more pressing tasks to be working on, and I don't want to waste any more of my time than I have to with someone who clearly has no say in the decision making process". Maddie was horrified that he'd actually articulated those words. How dare he be so rude? It was one thing to privately think it perhaps, but to speak to her in that manner was completely unacceptable. Just like that, the charming man who had walked in from the elevator was replaced by a business-like grump.

Charming, thought Maddie. She wanted to argue that Adam had, in fact, given her carte blanche over any decisions which needed to be made concerning the apartment, and that as his girlfriend she was effectively living here at the moment, so she was definitely more than an employee, but she didn't think it would make a difference now, and like Mr Harris, all of a sudden, she just wanted this inspection visit over and done with.

Russell Harris took a cursory glance around each of the rooms in the apartment which, despite the fact that the housekeeper had been in the previous day to clean, Maddie had worked hard that morning to ensure were sparkling and attractive. He was completely disinterested by her baking efforts, refusing her offer of a cupcake or cookie, which she had to restrain herself from ramming down his throat, considering his rude and arrogant behaviour, and when they returned to the lounge area less than five minutes after his arrival, he simply scooped up his coat, returned his tablet to his briefcase, and pressed the call button for the lift without so much as a word or glance in her direction.

Maddie felt the need to say something so asked him "Are you able to give me any indication of the retail or rental prices you would suggest that Mr Baynes markets this property at?".

Russell Harris glared at her, as if she'd asked the most impossible question replying curtly "No. I will be in touch with your boss" and with that he turned and entered the waiting elevator, then was gone.

"How rude!" Maddie said out loud as the lift doors closed behind her guest. "Clearly I need a different tactic with the others" she mused.

Maddie need not have worried. Helen Schwarz arrived as planned at two that afternoon, and unlike Russell Harris, she was clearly expecting Maddie and even knew her name.

"Miss Lane, very pleased to meet you. I'm Helen and I hope that I'm going to become your realtor. What a lovely apartment this is and wow, look at that amazing view!" Helen had wandered in the direction of the huge floor to ceiling windows which overlooked the Hudson River in the large loungeroom.

"Stunning isn't it?" Maddie replied, remembering how she herself, had stood mesmerised for several minutes upon first entering Adam's apartment and seeing the picturesque outlook.

"I would absolutely love to live in a place like this" Helen murmured wistfully "tell me, Miss Lane, why is it that Mr Baynes wants to leave this penthouse?". Maddie immediately developed a rapport with the realtor stood beside her, as they both gazed out over the huge river. Maddie explained her relationship with Adam, his plans to relocate to the UK to start up a new business, and the fact that ideally they wanted to be based back in England by the end of January, provided that Adam could get things organised at work by then, his big meeting with the Board of Directors being that afternoon.

Helen spent an entire hour wandering around the apartment with Maddie, pausing for coffee and a cupcake in the kitchen. She took detailed notes in a slightly battered and worn looking brown leather Filofax, and chatted amiably to Maddie throughout the entire process. Unlike with the previous agent, Maddie felt that Helen genuinely wanted to see every aspect of the apartment and was very keen to explore, to look in the various closets and to get an accurate picture of the property she would potentially be marketing. Upon concluding their lengthy tour of the apartment, Helen and Maddie sat down on the two sofas in the lounge and Helen produced some paperwork from her expensive looking Mulberry leather work bag.

"I'm going to be completely honest with you Maddie, I think you'd be mad to sell if there are still business interests here in New York for your partner, because one day you might want to return. Whilst it's not necessarily a family home, you could easily accommodate a family here with the space this property has, and it would be snapped up immediately as a rental, of that I have no doubt, so you would then be able to keep it as an investment. Now you probably know that when Mr Baynes purchased this property, it was through our agency and my brother dealt with him at the time".

This was news to Maddie. She had no idea who the agent was that sold the property to Adam, or that Helen's business was a family one, although the fact that her surname was the same as the agency name and the way she had behaved certainly served to reinforce that idea.

Helen continued "I believe the purchase price in November 2016 was just shy of six million dollars" Maddie's heart leaped, and she was so glad that she'd done her research or else Helen would have witnessed Maddie's very best goldfish impression at that information. "I would say that with the market as it is now, if you were selling, then we'd look to promote this property at offers in the region of twelve million".

Now Helen really did witness the goldfish impression "Twelve million? You mean it's value has doubled in those three years?" Maddie couldn't believe it.

Helen nodded encouragingly, adding "your partner got lucky when he bought this place, as the owner was relocating and desperate for a quick sale, so he offered the property at less than market value, but even still, prices have risen considerably and my prediction is that they will continue to do so. My advice would be to rent the property for a few years, particularly as you want to relocate quickly, and to reassess the sales market a little further down the line if you're certain that you don't want to return to the US. That is, of course, assuming that you don't need the capital from the property?".

Maddie didn't really know what to say to that question so opted for "I think Adam wants to keep his home and work separate, so he wouldn't be using capital from the apartment to fund the business, and I have my own home in the UK, so he doesn't need to sell immediately, as we have somewhere to live".

The rental income that Helen suggested as realistic was far above what Maddie would have anticipated. Helen advised that they market the property at ten thousand dollars per calendar month, which, although lower than her research had suggested, still seemed an extremely high figure to Maddie, but Helen said that she was very confident they could have tenants in place by the end of February at that price. Maddie promised that she would discuss things with Adam over the weekend, which he had assured her would be a weekend off work, and then get in touch with Helen again on the Monday morning. She did, after all, have one more realtor to see that afternoon, although she doubted that she would warm to the other one quite as much as she had to Helen.

17

Maddie's experience with the final realtor was much like that with Russell Harris. The booking had been with a JJ Lawrence, and Maddie had not known whether to expect a male or female agent through the elevator doors late that afternoon, but the young male whizz kid who had walked in seemed about as interested in her and the property as she was about her nieces' latest obsession with Spy Ninjas; some random YouTube phenomena that all the young children thought was amazing but about which she really couldn't have cared less. Like the first realtor, JJ only stayed in the apartment long enough to take a quick glance around, said that cookies and cupcakes were bad for you and he was vegan, sugar and caffeine free so couldn't eat them, or accept a coffee from her, anyway. He also refused to discuss prices with her, although didn't display quite as much disdain as the other man who had viewed the property, and simply said that company policy was to put their findings in writing to the owner rather than make an assessment on the spot. Assuming that Adam was still willing to give her autonomy over the process of marketing the apartment, Maddie knew that Helen would be the realtor she would be working with again, so didn't allow JJ's manner to upset her in the way that the same behaviour from Russell Harris had.

JJ hadn't long left the building when Maddie heard the ping of the elevator, announcing Adam's return from work. She was desperate to recount the events of her day to him, and equally keen to confront him on the question of his wealth, having gained an insight into just how much money he actually had now, but as they met in the hallway between the kitchen where she had been preparing dinner, and the lounge into which he had arrived, she realised that he was equally itching to impart news and information.

"Am I correct in thinking your meeting went well?" she asked, taking the bottle of champagne he was proffering and putting it in the large American style fridge, then searching unsuccessfully for a vase for the beautiful bouquet of flowers he still held in his hands. "Do you actually own a vase Adam?" she asked as she scoured each of the cupboards in the kitchen.

"Probably not!" he said as he placed them down on the counter top and scooped her into his arms "but it doesn't matter. We can buy one later when we go out to celebrate" and with that he kissed her soundly and she melted into his embrace.

Finally recovering her composure, after their long steamy kiss which literally took her breath away, Maddie asked again "So tell me about the meeting".

Adam explained that it couldn't have gone better. One of the Board members was looking to invest more in the company, following their previous conversations about expansion which was what had originally given Adam the idea that they could branch out into the UK. Now that he had somewhat scuppered this idea, deciding that he would prefer to start a new business from scratch with Ed, his colleague had asked to purchase seventy percent of the shares Adam held in the company, which would make Stephen Green the majority shareholder in Spruce Investments, and as he had recently resigned from his position in another company, thinking he would be increasing his stake in Spruce to allow for expansion, he was looking for an active role in the company and the Board had immediately agreed his appointment as CEO to replace Adam, once the transfer was complete.

Maddie struggled to take all this in. Having not yet managed to have the promised meeting with Rosalie, Adam's personal assistant at

Spruce, she realised that she had absolutely no clue what Adam's current stake in the company was worth, or how this new development would pan out.

"So, forgive my naivety, but as I've discovered today that you're far more wealthy than I ever actually realised, please would you spell all this out for me. I need to know what sort of figures we're talking about, and I need to know what this means for us, in terms of the new business and so on. If I'm really your personal assistant, and I'll admit to feeling more like chief cook and bottle washer at the moment, or your 'kept' girlfriend, then I really need to have a proper understanding of the business".

Adam took her by the hand, and led her into the lounge, where they sat face to face on one of the large black sofas. He had known that sooner or later he would need to explain to Maddie just how wealthy he was, and admit the success of his business ventures, but he liked behaving like an ordinary guy from Dorking. Sure, there had been times when he'd splashed his cash around, like when he'd taken her on a helicopter tour of the city, and when he'd upgraded her flight home to first class without telling her, not to mention when he had taken both Maddie and his parents out for an extortionately priced meal in a highly exclusive restaurant on Christmas Eve. That particular extravagance had backfired as he realised that neither his parents or his girlfriend had felt in the least bit comfortable during the meal and they were all desperate for that portion of the evening to end, as it wasn't a lifestyle they either wanted nor were accustomed to.

"Bottom line is that I'm a multi-millionaire" Adam started.

Maddie nodded. "I kind of worked that out for myself today when I discovered that you'd paid six million dollars in cash for this place, which incidentally is worth about double that now" Maddie commented.

"Wow, double. That's great interest on my investment" Adam said, somewhat nonchalantly.

Maddie couldn't believe that she'd just told him, albeit very off handedly herself, that his apartment was worth somewhere in the region of twelve million dollars and he'd barely batted an eyelid. "Just how multimillion are we talking Adam?" she asked.

"At last count, my net worth, taking into consideration all of the shares I have in Spruce and a couple of other ventures, plus the property that I own, was somewhere in the region of two hundred million US dollars. I earn roughly five million dollars a year at the moment, although I plough a lot of that back into the business". Adam sat and waited for this to sink in. Maddie just kept staring at him, not really sure how to react to this new information.

"Five million dollars a year" she said finally, "you actually earn five million dollars each year?". Adam nodded. He didn't want to make a big deal out of this, although he was astute enough to realise that for Maddie this sum of money seemed impossibly large. She was, after all, excited about receiving an inheritance of seventy-five thousand pounds, which to Maddie was a life changing amount of money, yet to Adam it was literally small change. "Like I said, I've ploughed most of what I earn back into the company, or to shares in other companies and properties which I own, but I take home about fifty-five thousand dollars a month for spending money and savings". Maddie continued to gaup at him as though he'd suddenly transformed into an alien creature. She had absolutely no comprehension of his worth, or what it would be like to have that amount of money. It was a world away from her experience. She thought back to his parents' home in Dorking, and the way he must have been brought up. None of this added up. He couldn't be that wealthy and still appear this normal. Could he?

Finally finding the words she needed, Maddie said "Okay, so you really do have a lot of money. More than I can ever imagine, but I still don't understand how".

Adam went on to explain how he'd made his fortune, buying and selling shares in businesses, developing Spruce from a small investment company in which he'd bought shares, into the multinational company that it had become under his leadership.

Adam was good at what he did, that was the crux of it, and whilst he was relatively unassuming about his wealth, he enjoyed the lifestyle he had, where the finer things could easily be bought and where he didn't ever have to worry about future security.

"I remember when I was a kid, and sometimes my mum and dad really struggled financially. There were times when Dad would get a bonus at Christmas, and that would pay for a holiday the next year, or finance redecorating the house and things like that, but other years they'd struggle to pay the bills each month, and mum would have to get part time work whilst we were at school to tide us over. I never wanted to be in that position, so I studied business, worked my way through University so that they wouldn't have to pay my living expenses because they couldn't have afforded that, and ultimately made a successful career out of what I do. I've tried to give money back to my parents over the years, as a thanks for what they've done for me, but they always refused to accept anything. When I made my first half million, I offered to pay off their mortgage, so that Dad could retire early, but they wouldn't take a penny from me. Like when I offered to pay for us all to go to Florida. They're insisting on paying for Jim and the kids, yet I can afford to pay for it all so much more than they can, but they won't have it. I guess its pride, and I get that, but I'd love to be able to repay them for all the sacrifices they made for me and Han when we were kids".

Maddie looked lovingly into Adam's eyes as he spoke, wondering if, like her, his parents were actually clueless as to exactly how much money he really had. As she gazed up at this man that she loved, she could genuinely see the passion and love that he had for his family, and for the first time since meeting him, Maddie finally realised just how important they were to him, despite his outward appearance of not giving them the time they deserved.

"You do realise that your family loves you despite your money, not because of it, don't you" Maddie commented.

Adam nodded. "I've come to recognise that in the past few weeks. I know that to them, and to you come to that, my money is unimportant, and that none of you want flashy homes or expensive meals, but instead you want me, and the lad from Dorking at that, rather than Adam Baynes CEO. I won't apologise for my money, because I've worked hard to earn it, but I do realise now that there are more important things in life and I do want to make changes, starting with relocating, which, incidentally, I should be able to do much sooner than I thought".

Seizing this snippet of information, Maddie asked "How so?".

Adam explained that having agreed to sell seventy percent of the shares he had in Spruce to Stephen Green, and with Stephen taking over his position as CEO, the transition would be much quicker than he had originally anticipated. Stephen was free to start work immediately, so they had agreed a one week handover period, meaning that Adam would be free to fly home with Maddie the following weekend.

"I've booked my seat on the plane and everything" Adam said proudly, then correcting himself "Well, Rosalie booked it for me, but I'm on that plane with you which is the important bit". Maddie was ecstatic. She didn't really want to return to England without him, but as she was supposed to be going to the theatre with Juliet and Fiona the following Sunday, a long-standing engagement which she didn't want to miss, she had been clear about only staying in New York for ten days. Adam was equally pleased to be heading home so quickly, although he knew there was a huge amount of work to be done in the meantime.

"I'm going to have to work long hours next week I'm afraid, and I know that I promised I wouldn't work this weekend, but I've got a couple of meetings lined up tomorrow because if I'm handing over the reins this soon, then there is a lot of work to do in a short space of time, but I'll be all yours from next Friday evening, and I'm definitely still taking this Sunday off. I also think we should go out and celebrate tonight, and I need to hear all about your day too, and how you got on with the realtors".

Maddie was still reeling from all the new disclosures of the evening, and not entirely sure how to respond, but, as if sensing her uncertainty, Adam caressed her face with his hands and said "I love you Madeline Lane, and I love that you're here with me as I start a new chapter of my life. I completely understand that this is all a bit overwhelming for you, and that perhaps I'm not exactly the person you imagined me to be, but I know that, thanks to you, I'm a better person. I really want to make this work between us, and I really want to make a success out of the business with Ed. Please say that you'll stay by my side. I honestly don't think I could do any of this without you".

There was still so much to say, and so many details to work out, but at that moment, Maddie felt more secure than she had done in months. She too, was very much in love with Adam, and whilst all the changes in her life were scary, the one thing she felt sure of was that together they could weather whatever storms life threw in their direction. Settling for actions rather than words, she kissed Adam gently and once again, they lost themselves in each other. Together, they could take on the world.

18

Subconsciously rubbing her stomach, knowing that two more children were quietly cooking away inside of her, Francesca stood by the kitchen window watching her husband try, with limited success, to rally each of their four existing children into his waiting Audi SUV. The family were heading to her brother's for the day, to celebrate her father's seventy fifth birthday, and although they felt a little guilty for stealing the limelight which should really belong solely to the birthday boy, Ed and Francesca had decided to wait for an appropriate moment during the family luncheon to impart the news of their rapidly increasing family. They had, on the way home from seeing the gynaecologist and discovering that they were expecting twins, considered telling at least their adoptive daughters that evening, but in the end had decided it was better to let the news sink in, and to give themselves twenty four hours to get used to the idea, before telling anyone.

The Marten family were extremely close. Francesca and Jeremy had lost their mother to cancer as teenagers, and within weeks Francesca's closest friend, Sally, the natural mother of the two teens Francesca and Ed now referred to as their daughters, had been orphaned. Sally had never known her father, as he had died when she was very young, and so her mother had brought her up alone, until like Juliette Marten, she had also lost her battle with cancer. Douggie Marten had immediately taken Sally under his wing, assuming guardianship of the seventeen year old girl, and treating her as one of his own children, without a second thought. Together, the four musketeers as they'd affectionately referred to themselves, had come to terms with their immense grief at losing two very important women in their lives, as both families had been incredibly close prior to the tragic circumstances that bound them together. Similarly, when Sally and her husband Tim had been killed in a freak car accident, the Marten family had rallied around their children, already considered to be very much a part of the family, and Francesca and Ed had not only assumed legal guardianship of the orphaned children, but later adopted them as their own.

Francesca couldn't be sure how her extended family would react to the news of two more babies, but she did know that no matter what happened, she would have their total and uncompromised support. The Marten family were renowned for being there for each other come what may, and she knew this would be no exception, but she and Ed were still reeling from the shock of finding out that she was expecting at the ripe old age of forty six, and she knew it would come as a shock to her loved ones too.

Once all the children had been coerced into the waiting vehicle, Francesca grabbed the bags of supplies from the kitchen worktop that she was taking to the party as their contribution, and made her way out to the car, locking the house behind her.

"Everyone ready?" asked Ed cheerily, to which he got a highly enthusiastic cheer from his sons and a less buoyant "yes dad" from the girls.

"Okay then, let's go party" Ed said in his best 'Barbie Girl' singing voice and both his wife and daughters chuckled at his rather poor Aqua impression.

"You do realise that this is a seventy fifth birthday celebration, don't you Dad?" Bronwyn asked somewhat sarcastically. She, for one, didn't anticipate it being quite as riotous an affair as the sixteenth and seventeenth birthday celebrations of her friends that she'd been used to attending over the past few months, and whilst she always enjoyed the Marten family celebrations, she didn't think today could really be classed as a party, as it was unlikely to be much different to their regular family lunches.

"I can't believe Grandad is seventy five today" chipped in Libby, adding "He really doesn't look or act like someone that old".

Francesca swivelled in her seat to face her younger daughter "Don't let Grandad catch you using the word 'old' to describe him" she warned. "He won't like that one bit!".

Douggie Marten was what could only be described as a young man, with lots of life experience. To look at him, you would be forgiven for assuming he were in his early sixties at most, and he was still as active as many men half his age, regularly playing squash with his son and son-in-law, and jogging every day. He had even participated in the London marathon four years previously, finishing in a very respectable four hours and forty seven minutes. He was very active, extremely healthy, and always denied his actual age, although his family obviously knew how old he really was.

Arriving at Jeremy and Fiona's house, Bronwyn was pleased to see her older cousin's car parked in the driveway. "AJ's here already" she announced, as though this was a particularly important piece of information which the family needed to be made aware of. As younger children, they'd always played well together, both sharing a love of sports. Now Adam, known to his friends as AJ, was at university studying Economics and Bronwyn, with her business brain, enjoyed long conversations with her cousin about the current financial climate, how best to manage money and what made businesses succeed and fail. They had a lot in common, and unlike with Riley who was almost exactly the same age as Bronwyn, it was as if she and AJ shared some sort of special connection.

Before Francesca and Ed had even stepped out of the car, all four of their children were inside the house and sharing tales of the previous week with their aunt, uncle, grandfather and cousins.

Ed looked at his wife and asked her "are you ready for this?"

Francesca looked into his eyes for a moment, finding comfort in his love and support and replied somewhat coyly "I'm ready as I'll ever be" and opened the car door.

Fiona was a fantastic cook, having previously been a professional caterer before giving up work to care for her four children, and therefore the meal was as delicious as always. Francesca marvelled at how, no matter when you went for a meal at Fiona and Jeremy's house, the food was always cooked to absolute perfection and looked exquisite too. She was capable of cooking plenty of decent tasting meals herself, having become very accustomed to catering for her own large brood, but the presentation was often lacking and usually at least one of the vegetables was either slightly over or slightly under cooked. This never seemed true of Fiona's cooking, and the cake she had made for her father-in-law's birthday, notably without any mention of the numbers involved, was equally amazing.

"You've done a tremendous job as always Fi" Francesca complimented her sister-in-law, "I honestly have no idea how you manage it".

Fiona laughed and returned "Well I have no idea how you manage to hold down such an intensive full-time job with four kids in tow, Ches. If you ask me, that's far more of an achievement than cooking a meal like this. I gave up on the idea of being able to work and run the home simultaneously years ago!".

Francesca looked in the direction of her husband, who gave a subtle nod. The youngest three children had been granted permission to leave the table to go and play in another room, which left the adults and five teenagers in the room. "Actually, I might not be working full time for much longer" Francesca began.

"Is this to do with Dad's new business?" Bronwyn asked, clueless to where this conversation was leading, but having been excitedly telling AJ all about the plans that Ed had with the other Adam who had entered their lives recently.

"No darling," Francesca answered, noticing the puzzled looks around the table and deciding it was best not to drag this out any longer, "it's got to do with the fact that I'm pregnant".

There was stunned silence around the room. No one had expected that bombshell to be dropped, and it certainly had the effect of stopping everyone in their tracks, as cutlery was laid down and glasses returned silently to the table.

Libby was the first to speak. "You mean you're having another baby mum?" she asked, as if needing Francesca to spell out the facts for her.

Francesca nodded then added "Yes… well, er… no… actually" stumbling over the words, she couldn't believe how hard she was finding this, with all eyes trained on her, willing her to continue. "You see, darling, it's not just one other baby".

Everyone looked quizzically at Francesca, as Ed clarified. "We found out yesterday that not only is Ches pregnant again, but we're having twins".

As the news sank in, the family gathered around the table erupted in congratulatory comments and everyone seemed to be thrilled at the unexpected news. Doug, Danny and Sally heard the commotion and returned to the dining room to find out what they were missing, not wishing to be left out, and Ed explained their news to the younger children. "Does this mean I'm going to be a big brother?" asked Danny very innocently.

"Yes son, that's exactly what it means. In four months time you're going to be a big brother".

Eagle eared as ever, Bronwyn picked up on the timeline and asked "hang on, you just said five months. When exactly can we expect these babies to put in an appearance and how come you're only just telling us now if they're coming that soon?". Francesca then had to explain to the family the circumstances and the fact that the babies would be joining them at the end of May.

Once the dust had settled, and everyone's questions had been answered, Francesca sought a moment alone with her father in the hallway. "Are you okay with all this Dad?" she asked, worried that he might be concerned at the amount of additional babysitting he was potentially going to have thrown at him in the coming months.

"If you're happy sweetheart, then I'm happy for you love" he replied, adding "and don't you worry. I might be an old man on paper, but I'm not beyond changing dirty nappies just yet, so your childcare is safe for a while to come yet!".

Francesca hugged him tightly. "Thanks Dad" she whispered into his ear. "I honestly don't know how we'd manage without you".

Douggie smiled to himself. "Well it's a good job I don't plan on you having to find out any time soon then, isn't it!".

19

By Sunday evening, when they returned from a fantastic day out in the city, Maddie and Adam had made numerous plans for the future. Having previously felt somewhat excluded from his business dealings, Maddie was thrilled when Adam suggested that she should accompany him to the office on the Saturday morning, and even happier when he left her alone in his office with a whole host of papers to peruse. Adam had finally admitted that the reason he'd kept Maddie away from the office previously, was that his assistant Rosalie had been less than enthusiastic about his idea of having her show Maddie the ropes of his business. Whether this was due to a form of resentment that Maddie was the cause of Adam leaving the company, or because she was simply too busy with all that his impending departure entailed to be walking someone through every procedure, Adam couldn't say, but by giving Maddie unlimited access to the office on Rosalie's day off, he ensured that Maddie could get a feel for things on her own.

Maddie had spent the whole of Saturday researching Spruce Investments and finding out exactly what it was that Adam did. She didn't pretend to understand the intricacies of the company, but she did establish that Adam was the majority shareholder, with an overall stake of sixty percent. Stephen Green, who was buying seventy percent of that stake from Adam, currently owned twenty five percent of the company, and each of the three remaining shareholders held five percent each. The company's estimated value was three hundred million dollars. That meant that Adam's total share was worth one hundred and eighty million dollars, and Stephen had a seventy five million dollar stake. In purchasing seventy percent of Adam's shares, for which he had offered Adam one hundred and twenty five million dollars, Stephen would own two thirds of the company, leaving Adam with shares to the value of around fifty four million dollars which equated to around eighteen percent of the total company value. This meant that he was still a major shareholder, and still entitled to a say in the decision making processes, which Maddie discovered would be likely to mean by-monthly trips to New York for business meetings, but he would free up enough funds to match the one hundred million pound stake that Ed planned to contribute to the new company.

Maddie couldn't help but feel like she was dealing in monopoly money looking at all the figures swimming around on the pages in front of her. She had never had to consider such enormous sums of money in the past, even when buying her house, or running her own small business, and found it incredible to think that Adam, and come to that Ed whom she didn't know particularly well, but who always seemed so down to earth and grounded, thought nothing about dealing in these sorts of figures.

As she surveyed the numbers for the umpteenth time, desperately trying to work out the conversion rates to pounds sterling using an online conversion tool on her phone, there was a knock at the office door and without even thinking, she called "Come in".

A very smartly dressed young man stood in the doorway and seemed a little taken aback to see her sat in Ed's chair at his large frosted glass desk.

"Sorry Ma'am, I was actually looking for Mr Baynes" said the young clerk, "I have some papers here for his signature".

Maddie explained that she was Mr Baynes' new personal assistant, and that she would be working with him when he relocated to England. This was obviously the wrong thing to say, as the man stood before her seemed even more clueless.

"Clearly the office grapevine here doesn't work as efficiently as the ones I'm used to" she quipped, explaining to the bewildered young man that Adam would soon be stepping down as CEO, and relocating to England, and that she was there for the day to assess his current business position and establish a plan for their future business. Worried that she'd broken some kind of confidentiality agreement, Maddie was hugely relieved when Adam returned and explained that the young intern, to whom she had imparted the news, had been off sick the previous day, and was therefore unaware of the imminent changes within the company, but that it wasn't actually a secret and that his departure was common knowledge amongst the staff as she'd previously believed it to be.

Having finally satisfied herself that she at least understood the amounts of money involved, and having acquired a list of contacts who might prove useful in the future, from an address book held on his office computer, to which he had also granted her access, Maddie felt that the day had been a productive one. She had also met Stephen Green, and was satisfied that he would actually follow through with his plan to acquire a large percentage of Adam's stake in the company, as he seemed extremely enthusiastic about both becoming the majority stakeholder, and about taking over as CEO.

That evening, Maddie had finally managed to discuss with Adam the information imparted by Helen Schwarz as well, as they'd been somewhat distracted in the bedroom on the Friday night, and together they had come to the decision to keep the apartment in New York, as they didn't need the funds from it. The healthy income that it was likely to generate would not only pay the costs involved in renting the property out and pay the lease on the flat in Canary Wharf, but also provide a substantial additional sum of money which could be used to pay rental on business premises for the new company. In keeping the apartment, they were also keeping their options open for the future, as should they want to return to the States at any point, they would have a ready made base. Maddie resolved to meet with Helen on the Monday morning to set the wheels in motion, and sincerely hoped that Helen's confidence that she could have the property allocated almost immediately, wasn't misplaced.

Sunday had been a more relaxed day. Maddie expressed a desire to visit Central Park again, and to explore more of its hidden depths, as being such a vast expanse with so many attractions hiding within it, she never tired of exploring the huge Park. Maddie also wanted another opportunity to ice skate at the Rockefeller Center, which Adam was more than willing to support her with, although he decided that he would watch from afar, not feeling brave enough to don skates for a second time, having been terrified when she'd taken him skating there a few weeks previously. They had walked from Tribeca to the Rockefeller early in the morning, calling in at Maddie's favourite Starbucks on route, so that she could say hello to one of the baristas whom she had got to know on previous visits to the city, and then she had skated whilst Adam checked his work emails on his phone and took numerous photographs of Maddie on the ice. From there they had continued up Fifth Avenue to the edge of Central Park, pausing to look in a few shops on the way, then they had taken a horse and carriage as far as the Museum of Natural History, from where they'd wandered uptown through the park, exploring parts of the park which Adam had never previously visited.

By the time they had reached the north east corner of the park, they had woven their way through several miles of greenery and were absolutely exhausted. Adam suggested that they should find the nearest subway station, and doing so, they made their way back to Times Square on the train. Knowing how much Maddie loved the theatre, Adam mooted the idea of trying to obtain last minute seats for a Broadway performance that evening. Maddie, never one to turn down a theatre visit, and feeling that she'd earned a reward after all her hard work the previous day, suggested the Lion King, as they saw a billboard advertising the show when they climbed up the stairs out of the subway, and as they got to the theatre they discovered that the evening performance that day was at 6.30pm, so less than an hour away. They secured two exceptionally good seats in the stalls, then dashed off to grab something to eat quickly before returning to watch the spectacular performance.

Maddie had seen the London theatre production of the highly acclaimed show previously, as well as both of the Disney films on which it was based, but to Adam the show was an entirely new experience. He was totally mesmerised by the actors in costume, and the spellbinding way that they use extra tools to move their costumes giving the illusion that they are real animals. The actors portraying Mufasa and Scar were particularly adept at moving their mechanical headpieces in such a way that the characters appeared to lunge at each other, and the puppetry used astounded him.

"I've honestly never seen anything like that in my life" he exclaimed as they left the theatre at the end of the performance. "It was absolutely amazing. One of the best shows I've ever seen. Thank you for suggesting it Mads".

She laughed. "You were the one who bought the tickets, and the one who suggested that we come to the theatre in the first place" she retorted.

"I know, but I'd never have picked that show without you" he replied.

It was as they finally settled down with a glass of wine on his huge sofas, that Maddie checked her social media accounts, having been too preoccupied until then to do so. "Oh wow!" she exclaimed, shooting a look over at Adam "Did you know this?".

Adam looked bemused, as he too scrolled through his Facebook page "know what Hun?" he asked half-heartedly.

"Ches is preggers!" Maddie almost shouted back.

"Sorry, what?" Adam asked, not fully understanding either Maddie's slang or the implications.

"Francesca Marten is pregnant. You know, Ches who we had dinner with last weekend. Ed's wife".

The penny dropped with Adam as he replied "oh" not really sure what this would mean.

Scrolling further through the post, and discovering more information, Maddie then added, "and not only are they expecting, but according to this post from Fi, it's twins!".

20

Adam hadn't seemed particularly perturbed by Ed's change in personal circumstances. "They've got four kids already Mads, I'm sure another one or two won't make that much difference" he'd said, but Maddie wasn't convinced. She had wanted Adam to contact Ed as soon as they'd found out, but as it was already nearly 10pm on a Sunday night in New York, it would have been three in the morning in the UK and even she had to admit that calling Ed at that time of day, when he'd clearly not been worried enough himself to call Adam, probably wasn't a sensible plan. That didn't stop Maddie lying awake half the night tossing and turning though. She didn't really know why she was worried, as after all, she knew that even without Ed's capital Adam had more than enough money to relocate to the UK and invest in some form of business venture, but she was also painfully aware how much Adam wanted Smithers, Baynes and Co to become a reality and Ed was the one with all the contacts in England that could make it happen.

When Adam dressed for work at 6am, she made him promise to telephone Ed at the earliest possible opportunity. He'd tried whilst she was making him a coffee, knowing that Maddie wouldn't rest until she knew for sure that Ed was still on board with the idea, but his friend's mobile had gone straight to voicemail. Adam knew that Ed was most likely in meetings and unable to take calls so had his phone switched off, but his being uncontactable only served to worry Maddie further.

"I'm sure everything's fine Mads, please don't worry" Adam had said as he left the apartment, kissing her gently as he waited for the elevator to collect him.

"I know" Maddie reasoned, "but I can't help being concerned because I know how much this all means to you".

Adam smiled. "You just concentrate your efforts on getting the rental of this place organised. Leave Ed to me". She waved him off then headed for the shower herself, wondering what time Helen Schwarz would be in her office.

Ed sat at his desk, trying desperately to focus on the conference call he was currently in the middle of, but failing miserably. He was trying to decipher which Japanese businessman's voice belonged to which client and it was proving quite a challenge over the telephone. He was also struggling with comprehending their strong accents and had no inkling from the tone of their voices which way the meeting would go. He much preferred face to face contact, he mused. If you were sat in a room with someone then you could read their body language, but over the telephone you just had a disembodied voice or voices to contend with and no real understanding of what that person was thinking or feeling. Promising himself that when he and Adam were running their own company, and calling the shots themselves, there would be far less business done via telephone and far more in real meetings, Ed suddenly remembered his promise to Francesca to tell Adam about the twins. Neither of them were friends with Adam on social media, but Maddie was connected with Francesca and their very vocal family members had been less than discreet, with the girls immediately posting on their social media pages that they were going to be big sisters again and both Fiona and Jeremy publicly congratulating them. It wouldn't be long before the news filtered through to Adam, and Francesca was concerned that he may get cold feet about their business venture, which was the last thing Ed wanted, although he wouldn't blame anyone for not wanting to partner him at the moment, because he realised that in zoning out of the meeting, he had probably just lost his company a few hundred thousand pounds. Bugger!

Once the conference call was finished, and having managed to repair some of the damage his lack of focus had caused, meaning that whilst the company hadn't gained as they should have from the meeting, they were no longer out of pocket, Ed decided that he really needed to call Adam and get that job ticked off the list. It was now two in the afternoon in London, meaning it was nine in the morning in New York and so Ed dialled Adam's office number, expecting to find him at his desk.

"I'm afraid that Mr Baynes is in a meeting at the moment and can't be disturbed" came a somewhat disgruntled female voice from the other end of the line.

"Okay, well do you know when he might be available. I need to talk to him relatively urgently" replied Ed, hoping that this tactic would get him past Adam's grumpy receptionist.

"I'm sorry Sir, but Mr Baynes has left strict instructions that he's not to be disturbed. Would you like me to put you through to another consultant?" Ed winced. He should have used Adam's mobile. It would have been far simpler.

"No, that's okay, I'd prefer to deal directly with Mr Baynes. Please would you have him call me when he's free. My name is Ed Smithers."

Rosalie put the phone down. She knew exactly who Ed Smithers was, and she had known who he was since the second she had answered his call, thanks to the state of the art caller display that the company's telephone system had. Moreover, she also had instructions from her boss that if either Ed or Adam's girlfriend Maddie were to call, they should be put through to him immediately, but Rosalie was still holding on to the vain hope that his departure from the company could be prevented. Adam hadn't left yet, and nothing had been signed to seal his departure. The way she saw it, that gave her five days to prevent the move and ensuring that Adam didn't speak to his English friends was only part of her plan. She could see that Adam had been in over the weekend, and that Stephen Green, her potential new boss had been here too, and she had been informed by the intern that Adam's girlfriend had been poking her nose in to the office affairs as well, meaning that any errors on paperwork could be blamed on the newcomer which would take the heat off Rosalie herself.

Smiling sweetly, as she knocked and entered Adam's office, where he and Stephen Green were deep in discussion, Rosalie passed Stephen some of the paperwork she had spent the morning carefully doctoring.

"Here you are Mr Green, these are the first set of papers which need your signature". Knowing that Adam trusted Rosalie implicitly, and being in the middle of a task which required their full attention, Stephen signed the papers without looking at them, just as Rosalie had hoped that he would. Her timing was impeccable. Hopefully the mistakes contained within these documents, which would cost the company somewhere in the region of fifty thousand dollars, would be enough to cast doubt over Mr Green's ability to run the company. That would buy Rosalie some time to convince Adam to stay on. She had nothing personal against Stephen, but she liked Adam, and not just as a boss, and she would do literally anything to keep him.

It was later that afternoon when the mistakes were uncovered, after Rosalie subtly suggested to another colleague that she didn't feel Mr Green was in the right headspace to run the company, and casting doubts over the reasons behind his departure from his previous post. She was good friends with his old executive assistant, and she knew that in truth there was nothing untoward in his leaving, he had just wanted a new challenge, but she also knew that the rumour mill could work wonders if a seed of doubt was sown. By four in the afternoon, Adam was frantically running around trying to reverse the damage that had been done. Stephen couldn't understand why everyone seemed to have suddenly turned against him, and Adam couldn't comprehend how Rosalie had let such a large error slip through the net.

Deciding to confront her, after his attempts at damage limitation had failed, Adam asked "Why didn't you say anything before you got

Stephen to sign those papers? I'd have thought you were more than capable of spotting a huge error like that?".

Rosalie knew she had to be careful. Adam knew her well and she didn't want to let her façade slip in front of him.

"I'm sorry, I was so busy because there is a lot of additional work at the moment, and therefore I simply didn't have the time to check as meticulously as I usually would. I did notice some discrepancies, but I assumed that they were deliberate due to the changes the company is experiencing at the moment".

Adam wasn't convinced. It all seemed a little convenient. Rosalie had been very unhappy when he's explained his departure to her, and she had been behaving uncharacteristically ever since. He now knew, having finally spoken to Ed who had called him on his personal mobile a few minutes earlier, that Rosalie had been refusing to allow him to take Ed's calls all day. Maddie had also reported a similar problem, via a text message, after not being able to get past Rosalie to speak with him in person, to update him on her dealings with the Estate Agent.

Discussing the situation with Maddie that evening, Adam voiced his concerns. "You really think she sabotaged the transaction deliberately?" Maddie asked incredulously.

"Unfortunately, yes, I actually do think that" Adam replied solemnly. "I've always trusted Rosalie implicitly, but at the moment her behaviour is a huge cause for concern".

Maddie did her best to reassure Adam that surely Rosalie wouldn't be that devious, although having not met the woman, it was very hard to defend her actions, and offered to come in with Adam the following day to see if she could be of any assistance.

Adam then relayed to Maddie the conversation which he'd finally had with Ed that afternoon. Ed was confident that his impending return to the parenthood of tiny babies was not going to compromise their business arrangement, and reassured Adam that he was completely committed to their new venture, and that he had even managed to liquidate close to forty million pounds, which, together with the money Stephen had promised Adam for his Spruce shares, was enough to fund their start-up venture, although ideally they both wanted to put one hundred million pounds into the business, and be equal partners.

21

Mavis handed Jim a flask of coffee, and a Tupperware container full of sandwiches, snacks and fruit cake, as he dashed out of the house early on Tuesday morning.

"Sustenance to wish you good luck" she'd said as he gratefully took the box from his mother-in-law.

"Thank you so much for this Mavis, and for all your support with the kids. You really are a superstar" he replied, blipping the lock on his car as he waved goodbye.

Jim knew that he was extremely fortunate to have the love and assistance that Mavis and Peter continued to provide. They had arrived early the previous evening, just as he and the children returned home from work and school respectively, and Mavis had produced a huge casserole which she'd prepared earlier for their dinner, and boxes full of homemade cakes and treats for all of them. She had then insisted that he relax for the evening, leaving her and Peter to worry about the boys' homework, and getting them ready for bed and she'd even done his ironing for him, ensuring that he had a pristine shirt to wear the following morning.

He was very nervous as he drove towards Weybridge, but also excited. Knowing that successfully securing this new job would take him and the children back to Surrey, where they would have that support from Mavis and Peter on tap, was spurring him on. He had never been good at change, yet 2019 had proven to be a year filled with new challenges, many of them not changes for the better. He was determined that any changes in 2020 would be on his terms, and that the new equilibrium he would establish for himself and the boys would be full of positivity. Above everything else, he wanted the boys to be happy, but he would also quite like the chance to be happy again himself, and the more he thought about it, the more he realised that he couldn't ever be truly happy in Brighton without Hannah. Neither could he return to his old life in Leatherhead, not that this was an option as the company had relocated so was no longer there to return to, but he needed to forge a new normal for them all, somewhere where he was close enough to Hannah's family, but different enough to be about him and the boys and not tainted by memories, both good and bad, which made him feel permanently melancholy. It wasn't that he wanted to forget Hannah. On the contrary, he was determined to keep her memory alive for the children, and there was no doubting that Jamie had her genes; you only had to look at him next to his uncle and grandfather to see that. No, he wanted to remember the happy times, but let go of the sadness, and a new challenge at work might just give him the impetus that he needed to move on with his life.

Mark Edwards greeted Jim in reception and offered him a coffee which Jim gratefully accepted. He had already drunk the coffee that Mavis had packed him off with, whilst sat in traffic on the M25, and he functioned much better after two or three cups in a morning, yet on that day he had only had time to drink the one in the flask. Mark provided the promised coffee, then led the way up to his office, and Jim was surprised to find that he was the only candidate visiting that day. Mark explained that, of all the people they had interviewed the previous week, Jim had been the only person that they had wanted to review, and therefore provided that all went well today, the job would be his. Jim was astounded that such promises would be made so early in the day, but it also buoyed him up to think that he was actually in with a real chance of success.

Throughout the morning, Mark set Jim a variety of tasks to complete which were of the same ilk as those he would be required to undertake in the new role. Jim was asked to analyse one of the new products offered by Claxton Pharmaceuticals, and pit the product against similar products offered by rival companies. As organising a marketing campaign for something almost identical for Sphere had been one of his tasks at work the previous week, Jim found this very easy, and already had a sound knowledge of both the Claxton version and other similar products on the market. He set out a marketing plan for the new product which clearly impressed Mark, and was also able to articulate all the advantages and disadvantages of each product across the different brands.

In the afternoon, after being given lunch in the staff canteen at Claxton, rendering the lunchbox provided by Mavis unnecessary, Mark explained to Jim that they were now going to visit Parkside Surgery in Hampton Wick, which would be one of the practices that Jim would be working with *when* he joined Claxton Pharmaceuticals. Jim immediately picked up on the use of the word 'when' over 'if', but he tried desperately not to get his hopes up, as there was still nothing in writing and no guarantees.

Arriving at Parkside Health Centre, Mark told Jim that whilst some business came their way from this particular surgery, it was one where they were still trying to win over the Practice Manager and senior partner. "Sandi Morris runs this place with an iron hand" Mark explained, "and our products tend to be slightly more expensive than our competitors', which means that she's not willing to allow GPs to prescribe them unless she can be sure they are more beneficial. Your job, is to convince her, and possibly her boss Dr Marten, that Hydrocloraquil is better than any of the other alternatives currently on the market".

Jim was taken aback. He had not anticipated needing to actually convince anyone face to face today, but then he had done his research and he was confident that he knew his stuff, so he said "Okay, I'll give it my best shot".

All of the GPs were in surgery, and Parkside was clearly a very busy and well used practice, with a number of clinics running in addition to their doctors' appointments. There was a podiatry clinic, an anti-natal clinic, an asthma clinic and a diabetes clinic all taking place during the time that they were there, and there were ten doctors all running surgeries. The place was buzzing, and Sandi was clearly very busy, but she did make them feel welcome.

Jim ran through the same spiel that he'd prepared for Mark earlier, adding in costings which Mark was unaware he knew, highlighting the benefits of their Hydrocloraquil option over that of the competitors, and in doing so, found himself slating the Sphere brand, which sat uneasily with him, as technically they were still his employers, but he knew that there was a lot at stake and didn't want to blow his chances of this job. To his complete amazement, by the end of their meeting, Sandi had not only agreed to allow her GPs to prescribe their brand of the medication, but she had also promised to consider more of the Claxton brand products in future and said she was looking forward to working with him.

Walking out to the car, Mark took Jim's hand and shook it warmly.

"Well done Jim. You did an absolutely brilliant job in there. She's the toughest nut we have to work with, and you had Sandi Morris eating out of your hands. If you want it, this job is yours".

Jim thanked Mark, and said that yes, he would like the job, although needed to give a month's notice with Sphere and therefore wouldn't be able to start immediately.

"No problem, we'll head back to the office now and make a start on the paperwork and we can decide on a mutually acceptable start date for you. How does that sound?".

Although Jim said "Great, sounds absolutely great!" out loud, in his head he was thinking that it sounded like a brilliant opportunity but also completely scary as he was about to upheave his family for the second time in the space of a year and about to begin a completely new career path, because face to face meetings like the one he'd just sailed through were not something he'd ever had to do before, and he couldn't help feeling that perhaps it was a case of beginner's luck and he wouldn't be that successful in the future.

Back at the office, he and Mark agreed a start date of Monday 2nd March. That meant that he could work out his notice at Sphere, potentially move himself and the boys to Surrey during the school February Half Term break, and still have a week to get the children settled in their new school, before starting work the following Monday. This obviously assumed that they would find somewhere suitable to live, and more importantly find suitable schools for the boys, because although Mavis and Peter had very kindly offered to accommodate the family, Jim really wanted the opportunity to start afresh without relying on his in-laws.

Returning home that evening, to yet another lovely homecooked meal lovingly prepared by Mavis, Jim felt happier than he had in a long time. He typed up his letter of resignation on his laptop, and then immediately began searching for schools and houses online. This was the start of a new chapter, and he was determined to make 2020 a much better year for the McDonald household.

22

"Okay Sand, let me get this straight. You didn't like the last rep from Claxton so we were never allowed to prescribe their medication, but the new guy is hot so you've decided we should use them for everything from now onwards?" Francesca laughed as she breakfasted with her colleague the morning after Sandi's meeting with Mark and Jim.

"I didn't put it exactly like that Ches!" Sandi argued "but I do think that we should consider their brand of Hydrocloraquil because it will definitely be better for the patients, and if their new rep is hot then that's just an added bonus". Francesca struggled to restrain her seemingly uncontrollable urge to giggle and poke fun at her friend.

"What, pray tell, do you know about the differences between brands, other than the costs? You've never had any clue before, and you've always told me that the cost was the most important factor because there couldn't be that much difference between the different brands of medications containing the same active ingredients".

Sandi knew Francesca was right, but Jim had been very convincing outlining all of the various pros and cons which she now tried, without much success to relay to Francesca.

Sandi, at 39 years of age, was a little younger than Francesca, but unlike her friend and boss, she was hugely unlucky in love.

Continually searching for Mr Right, Sandi went on endless dates, either with men she met through work, those she'd hooked up with in bars, or on dates set up online through Tinder, Bumble and other apps, yet she never seemed to manage to get beyond the third date with anyone. Sandi envied Francesca's family life, and she had always been a huge part of the other lady's children's lives, living her dreams of motherhood through being an honorary auntie to Bronwyn, Libby, Doug and Danny. Sandi couldn't be happier for Francesca now, knowing that twins were on their way in just a few short months' time, but she also felt a twinge of jealousy as she would have dearly loved for it to be her that was expecting this time, rather than Francesca.

She also knew that Francesca's need for maternity leave would cause her some headaches at work. As practice manager, it was Sandi's role to balance the books of the Health Centre, and to ensure the smooth day to day running of the surgery. Whilst the younger, single GPs were more than happy to cover evenings and weekends, allowing Francesca and the other more senior GPs who had young families, the chance to spend time away from work at these times, all of their doctors had full lists, and therefore at least one locum would need to be employed to cover Francesca.

For Francesca's first maternity leave, they had more time to prepare as Francesca's pregnancy was made common knowledge at twelve weeks, meaning that the registrar that the practice was training was asked to stay on and take over. For the second, when pregnant with Danny, two of their semi-retired, and therefore part time, GPs had agreed to return to full time work for the duration of her leave. In both cases, the cover had been seamless, and patients were very happy, but this time would be more challenging. For starters, the registrar that they had just finished training was already covering Dr Samson's maternity leave, and as Julie had only left at Christmas, with the plan of taking a full year out for her first baby, the timing wouldn't work. Add to that the fact that all of the current GPs worked full time, it meant that unless they could coerce Dr Derek Woods back from retirement, which she felt was highly unlikely seen as how he was off travelling the world, they would need to find a locum.

"Anyway, moving on" Sandi began, desperate to change the subject and prevent further ridicule, "we need to discuss the topic of your impending maternity leave and who the hell we're going to get in to cover you". Francesca had been thinking about this too. It was not going to be easy to find someone suitable at such short notice, but as the babies were due to be delivered on or soon after 20th May, and as it was already the 15th January, they had very little time to find suitable cover, especially as after talking it through with her family, Francesca had decided that ideally she'd prefer to take her leave from the school Easter holidays, enabling her to spend some quality time with the other children, and then rest and fully prepare herself, before the twins arrived. That would mean finishing work on 3rd April and that was only eleven weeks away. With her previous two pregnancies, she had returned to work part time just six months after the children were born, relying on family support from Ed, who had worked from home three days per week, and her father and sister-in-law to cover her whilst she was working, but with Ed's new business venture, he was unlikely to be able to offer the same sort of time to the family when the twins were born as he had with Doug or Danny, and it really didn't seem fair to expect her father to cope with twin babies when he was seventy five years old. She knew that the girls would help, Libby especially being extremely good with young children, but she also knew that they were both facing important times in their studies with Libby in Year 9 having just embarked on the first year of her three year GCSE courses, and Bronwyn being in the first year of sixth form.

"Did you have any thoughts as to who we might approach?" Francesca asked, hoping that Sandi would already have the answer lined up, in what she'd come to refer to as true Sandi style, often solving potential problems before they arose.

"Sorry Ches, I'm totally stumped. I thought about Dr Lawson, as all the patients love her, but she only wants to work one or two days each week, and besides, if we used her then we'd be stuck for a locum to cover sick leave, so she's out. The only other option that I've thought of would be Derek, but I can't see him giving up his travels for six months or more, can you?". Francesca shook her head.

Derek had been her mentor when she'd joined the practice as a registrar, and when he had retired three years previously, with a view to travelling the world with his wife, she'd bought his share of the practice, making her the most senior of all the partner GPs and the biggest shareholder in the practice.

"I guess we have no choice but to advertise then?" Francesca half asked, half stated. "Unless any of the other practices locally have trained registrars they're willing to let go of for a while?".

Now it was Sandi's turn to shake her head. She had already approached all of the other practices in their confederation, and none of them was able to either recommend anyone suitable, or better still provide cover themselves.

"Looks like advertising is our only hope then" sighed Francesca. "You probably don't want to hear this, but I'd like to take a year off this time too" she added, deciding that it was better to be upfront now, if Sandi was placing an advertisement.

"A year! Are you sure?" Sandi questioned. She'd anticipated Francesca wanting less time out now that she was the most senior partner, not more.

As Francesca explained to Sandi why she felt the need to take the additional time; her age, the fact that it was twins, the fact that she wouldn't be able to rely on Ed so much, the need to be there for her other children as well as the new babies and so on, Sandi knew that it was the right decision, although she honestly couldn't see Francesca keeping away that long.

"I'll still come in weekly and meet with you" Francesca assured her, "and I can do the management side of things from home, but I just can't see me dedicating time to my patients as well as my family".

As Sandi drafted the advertisement for the maternity cover that morning, she reflected on all the changes she had witnessed over the years. She loved her job as Practice Manager, and since taking control of the medical side of things, Francesca had given her far more autonomy over the running of the rest of the health centre, meaning that her job had grown and she now not only managed the receptionists, but was in control of a team of staff who did a variety of different jobs. She was pleased that Francesca didn't intend for there to be managerial changes during her absence, but she couldn't help but wonder whether this was the beginning of Francesca stepping down from her role as a GP. If that were true, it would be a sad loss to the surgery, and there would be a lot of very unhappy patients. Sandi too, didn't know whether she would be willing to work for another employer. The transition between Derek and Francesca had been easy, as Francesca was already a senior partner before Derek left, and she had done much of the day to day running of the practice well before buying him out, but if Francesca left, then Sandi couldn't see any of the other GPs stepping in to her shoes. The only one with real potential to do so was Julie Samson, and as she was also in the process of baby making, her first child due literally any day, she was no more likely than Francesca to want to take over the running of the surgery. Maybe it was time for Sandi to look at other possibilities for her career. She wouldn't go yet, not until Parkside's future was secure, as she loved the place too much to see everything they'd worked for fall into decline, but if Francesca were to take a more permanent back seat, then maybe it would be time to move on herself.

"Food for thought" murmured Sandi to no one in particular.

23

Maddie had spent most of the week working alongside Rosalie in Adam's office, and it was blatantly obvious that something was very wrong. Maddie had managed to correct countless minor errors on pieces of paperwork, each one lacking significance alone, but the combined effect would have been disastrous for both Spruce as a company, and Adam as an individual. Rosalie made no effort to hide her disdain at Maddie's presence, but as Stephen Green had welcomed the newcomer into the office, agreeing with Adam that with two of them running the company alongside each other, having a dedicated personal assistant for each of them would make Maddie a valuable asset, Rosalie was left with no option but to accept the other woman's presence in her part of the office. Adam had even arranged for an additional desk to materialise from somewhere, enabling Maddie to have her own space and to actually feel worthy and valued.

If asked, Maddie could not have explained exactly why she had failed to flag any or all of Rosalie's mistakes to Stephen, technically her employer this week, as it had been deemed more appropriate that she work with him and not Adam, or even why she had said nothing to Adam at home, but something told her that she needed to give Rosalie the benefit of the doubt. Maddie knew that Rosalie had been a loyal employee with Spruce for many years, long pre-dating Adam's involvement with the firm, and she knew that her proven track record would be hard to dispute, should Maddie actually raise a concern. She was, however very concerned, and she was watching her new colleague like a proverbial hawk, cross checking every aspect of her work, thereby effectively doubling her own workload.

Rosalie meanwhile, was becoming increasingly frustrated. This English woman that she was being forced to work with was not only being unbelievably nice to her, as if she wanted them to be friends, but she was also thwarting every attempt she made to disrupt the transfer of control from Adam Baynes to Stephen Green. She had expected Adam's girlfriend to be a naïve, and quite frankly bumpkin like, girl with no real experience. Researching Maddie's past, she had discovered that Maddie was a trained chef, whose own small catering business had folded some years earlier, leading her to accept a post as personal assistant to someone who was effectively just a glorified hotel manager, managing a small chain of four hotels in the South East of England. Maddie's astuteness and flair for business had therefore surprised her, and unfortunately for Rosalie, nothing seemed to slip past the office interloper, therefore all the deliberate little errors she was making in an attempt to discredit Stephen, were being picked up by the little madam working with her, and she was being forced to correct them.

It was Thursday afternoon when Maddie finally uncovered something which she knew she could not hide from Adam or Stephen. The transfer of stock documents arrived back from the legal team, just as Rosalie left the building for her lunch break. Maddie opened the papers in her colleague's absence, and was absolutely horrified to see that the amounts detailed were completely incorrect. It wasn't as if a number had been omitted by mistake, or that this could be in any way blamed on human error. These figures were complete fabrication. Wanting to be in possession of all of the facts before taking the evidence to Adam, Maddie contacted the legal team and asked them to send through any documentation that they had regarding the transfer. Within half an hour, Maddie was looking at several documents, including memos and emails from Rosalie, all stating the incorrect figures. Recreating these documents, with all the entailed legalities, would be time consuming, and therefore this would undoubtedly delay the transfer and make it impossible for Adam to return to the UK with her the following evening as planned.

Taking a deep breath, and ensuring that she had everything to hand, she knocked on the door which separated her own part of the office from Adam's luxurious corner office, and mentally braced herself for what she felt obliged to tell them. Savvy to the last, not only did Maddie have all the documentation regarding the transfer in her possession when she entered Adam's office, but she had also kept copies of all of the other documents she had needed to correct. Armed with all of the evidence, Maddie explained the situation to Adam and Stephen.

Adam was shocked that Rosalie would do such a thing, but having had his suspicions earlier in the week, he was not entirely surprised. He expressed his displeasure that Maddie had waited so long to bring all of this to their attention, pointing out the potentially disastrous situation the legal documentation could have caused, but Maddie explained that she had wanted to be completely sure, and she had made certain that no harm had been done, double checking every aspect of Rosalie's work throughout the three days that she'd been there, something for which both Adam and Stephen were very grateful.

Making the decision that he couldn't possibly fly back to England that weekend as planned, Adam asked Maddie to change his flight, delaying his return to the UK by one week. Stephen also asked whether she would consider staying in the US beyond the weekend herself, and Maddie agreed that she would remain, but only for one additional week as she had an important family party to attend the following weekend and there was no way that she would miss being with her niece on Milly's fifth birthday. She would, however, call Juliet and Fiona and suggest they find someone else to go and see The Magnificent Music Hall Matinee with them this coming Sunday afternoon at the theatre, as she would no longer be home in time.

As Maddie called the airline to try and transfer the bookings, another anomaly presented itself. Adam was convinced that Rosalie had booked him on the same return flight to Heathrow as she herself was due to take that Friday evening, yet the airline had no record of a booking in his name for that flight, only hers. Indeed, the airline could not find any evidence that any flight had ever been booked in

Adam's name at any point in the future. Evidently Rosalie was determined to scupper his attempts to return home.

By the time Rosalie returned to the office, several other misdemeanours had been uncovered, as Adam, Stephen and Maddie all delved into all aspects of her work from the previous three weeks. It appeared that since the end of December, when Adam had first stated his intention to make amends with Maddie and his family, and intimated that this may well involve relocation to England, Rosalie had been plotting to dissuade him from the idea.

"Madeline! What are you doing at my desk?" Rosalie demanded, upon returning from her rather elongated lunch break.

"I'm trying to establish why you seem hell bent on sabotaging Adam's return to the UK, if you must know" Maddie retorted, having now lost all patience and compassion with the self-important lady stood before her.

"You have no right to be going through my personal documents, now move away from my desk immediately". Maddie knew that she should leave the confrontation to Adam and Stephen, but she was furious with this woman and simply couldn't help herself.

"I think you'll find that you no longer work here actually, after all your sabotage attempts. How dare you try and swindle Adam and this company? Who do you think you are?".

Taken aback, Rosalie tried to salvage the situation "I don't know what you're talking about, sabotage is a very strong accusation and I could sue you for defamation. There is clearly some mistake. I have every respect for Mr Baynes and I am a long serving and loyal employee of this company. You are wrong!".

At that very moment, Adam and Stephen, hearing the raised voices from the outer office, appeared at the adjoining door.

"Rosalie. My office. Now." Adam demanded, in a somewhat menacing tone. Maddie was slightly taken aback, having never heard

Adam speak like that to anyone. He was usually very calm and so friendly, but she could almost see the metaphorical steam coming out of his ears as he spoke. Even Stephen appeared to be cowering in the background.

A few minutes later, Adam's voice calmly came over the intercom requesting that she call for security. Maddie did as he bade, and within seconds two burly men in uniform appeared in her office. Knocking and entering Adam's inner sanctum, she led the way for the security guards who were instructed to supervise Rosalie collecting all her personal belongings and then escort her off the premises, retrieving her security passes as they did so. Adam then instructed Maddie to contact the IT department and have all staff passwords changed and all security codes reconfigured. He also asked her to send a memo to all staff working for the company to explain that there had been a serious confidentiality breach. In addition, Maddie was to reissue instructions for the legal documentation, this time with the correct figures, and to continue scouring Rosalie's computer and desk for any as yet uncovered problems.

It was very late that evening when they finally returned to Adam's apartment, satisfied that there was no significant damage done by the other woman.

"What made her do it?" Maddie asked, trying to comprehend the uncharacteristic behaviour and devious actions.

"She said something about doing it for me, because she thought I was mad to want to live in what she described as 'a tin pot island like England' when there were so many more opportunities here in the States, and she said that uprooting myself and moving half way across the world for a woman I'd only just met was crazy, but the thing is, as I'd already tried to explain to her, I love England. It's home. Sure, I've been successful here, but in well over three years, I've never actually been happy, not until I met you anyway" Maddie smiled at the compliment.

"I get that to her, the idea of living in England has no appeal, and for someone clearly as clever and as driven as she is, maybe it does seem like a backward step to leave a company which I've built up in to a huge success to start all over again, but I want that challenge, and I want to be near mum and dad and the boys and most of all, I want to see where things can go with us. The bottom line is that, although I could find challenges work wise here in New York, the people I love are all in England, so that's where I need to be. I thought that as a mother herself, she'd understood that before, but obviously not".

Maddie felt sorry for Adam. He clearly felt let down by his trusted assistant, and obviously the delays that she had caused were frustrating to say the least, but looking on the bright side, at least Maddie no longer felt so useless. Today, she had more than proven her worth to Adam in his business, and she had also very effectively demonstrated her ability to problem solve and identify concerns. Between working as PA to Adam and Stephen, and finalising the plans to rent out the apartment, Maddie was going to be extremely busy in the coming days.

24

"Mate, is it true?" Dave asked Jim as soon as he arrived at work on the Friday morning. Jim had spoken to his boss first thing on the Wednesday morning, but hadn't actually handed in his resignation letter until late the previous afternoon, once he'd received the official job offer and contracts from Claxton via email. Despite the fact that he had not informed anyone other than his boss of his impending move, suddenly it seemed that everyone in Sphere knew of his departure. Clearly the office grapevine was still extremely effective.

"Yes Dave, time for a change mate" Jim said, going on to explain, in part at least, his reasons for moving on. "I need a fresh start for me and the lads after everything that's happened in the past twelve months, and I need to be back nearer to the in-laws because the boys need their extended family around them. Han's brother is relocating back to the area too, moving home from New York, so now seemed like a good time". Dave was saddened to hear that his colleague was leaving, as they'd worked together for well over ten years now, with adjoining cubicles in the Sphere offices, but he understood Jim's reasons, and was extremely happy for Jim that he had been able to secure a great job so quickly.

"I couldn't believe it mate. I only applied the day I came back after Christmas, and they offered me the job this week. It's slightly different to what we do here, in that there's lots more face to face with the medics, but it's all the same skill set required in terms of product knowledge and competitor edge".

As the day progressed, more and more of his colleagues stopped by Jim's cubicle to congratulate him, including several he didn't think even knew his name. He felt honoured that so many people made the effort to seek him out, and was humbled by the number of colleagues who expressed their sadness that he was leaving. Obviously, he had made more of an impression during his time at Sphere, than he had first thought.

Jim had agreed with his boss that he would remain in post until the 31st January, then he would take some of the leave that he was owed by the company to account for the remainder of his notice period. This suited Jim as it gave him two weeks prior to the school holidays to gradually pack up their belongings before the planned move in half term. He had also agreed a half day that afternoon, as he had two estate agents coming to view his house, in preparation for putting it on the market. He didn't anticipate the house selling particularly quickly, and suspected that he would need to rent a property in Surrey for them to live in during the interim period, but he was planning on going house hunting that weekend. Mavis had said that she would go with him, and Peter was going to take care of the children. Mavis had tried to persuade him to move in with them until he could buy somewhere, but whilst the idea had a certain appeal, knowing that all the cooking, cleaning and childcare would be taken care of, he really wanted to stand on his own two feet, so had declined the generous offer. He was, however, eternally grateful that Mavis and Peter had stayed on throughout Wednesday and that she'd cleaned the house from top to bottom for him, as it was now in a much more presentable state for viewings, and the boys had been warned that they absolutely must keep it tidy until a sale was secured.

Jamie and Robbie had taken the news of the move well. Jamie had asked whether he could go back to his old school, where he had vague memories of other children, but Peter had helped Jim to explain that whilst they would be living closer to Nana and Grandad again, they wouldn't be living in the same town as their old house or old school. Robbie had then asked whether they would still be going on holiday to visit Mickey Mouse, if they were moving house, and Jim had assured both boys that the planned trip to Florida wouldn't be affected by the other changes in their lives, and it would give them all something to look forward to in the summer.

That afternoon, whilst waiting for the estate agents to arrive, Jim logged on to the Surrey County Council School Admissions website and searched for available school places in and around Weybridge. He had organised viewings of a variety of properties, both for sale and for rental, within a five mile radius of the Claxton Pharmaceuticals base at Brooklands, and the children's school location would play a key factor in deciding which, if any, of the properties he should consider moving into. Several of the schools rated 'Good' and 'Outstanding' by Ofsted seemed to be lacking in availability, but there were two schools in the locality with available places and checking them out online, Jim was reasonably impressed. He emailed both schools, explaining his position and requesting meetings with the Head Teachers, then logged off his laptop just as the doorbell sounded.

The first estate agent was a man in his early fifties who, whilst appearing very smarmy and absolutely wreaking of smoke, seemed to have a good heart. Jim explained the reason for his move, omitting the details of Hannah's death, just stating that his wife had passed away the previous year so he was relocating back to Surrey in order that his sons could be closer to her family. The kindly gentleman viewed each room in the house, making copious notes on a large lined notepad, then sat down in the lounge with Jim.

"I'll be honest with you Jim, if I can call you Jim?" Jim nodded in the affirmative. "If you want a quick sale, and I totally understand why you do, then your best bet would be to set an asking price of around three hundred and twenty five thousand, and expect to get around the three hundred mark". Jim baulked slightly. He and Hannah had paid three hundred and twenty when they'd moved, and to make a loss was not really something he had anticipated. "I know it seems low, and I know you bought it for three twenty, but the market is pretty stagnant at the moment. It should pick up as the year goes on, but its far more common for people to buy in seaside towns in the

Spring and Summer, than in the middle of winter, I'm afraid". Jim could see his point, and completely understood what he was saying, but the news certainly dampened his mood. Maybe he should consider living with Mavis and Peter after all, and then he could rent this place out for six months and put it on the market in June. He had a lot more thinking to do before he could make an informed choice.

The second agent who visited the property that afternoon was the same middle-aged chap who had sold Jim and Hannah the house. He was surprised to hear that they were moving on again so soon, but when Jim explained the circumstances suddenly a memory clicked in his mind.

"Oh Jim, I'm so sorry. I read about your wife's passing in the paper. Such a tragedy and just around the corner from my office it was too. I completely understand why you'd want to move away after that". Whilst not enjoying the reminder of the accident, Jim was relieved that at least the man understood his reasons for relocating, and Bob Willis was actually far more positive about securing a sale than the previous agent.

"I can't promise you'll make a profit Jim" he'd said, "but I'll do my very best to ensure that you don't make a loss if you sign on with us. Being located close to the school, we get a lot of trade in our office from families, and I reckon if I put this house on at three hundred and fifty thou today, I could have footfall through the door by tomorrow afternoon, and hopefully a decent offer very soon. I can rush it through, as we still have all the details on file from when we sold it to you, and considering the circumstances, I'll offer you a reduced fee too. If I sell it for more than three two five, give me a grand in commission, and if it's less, I won't take a penny. How does that sound?".

To Jim that sounded absolutely perfect. He remembered how he and Hannah had stumbled across Bob's agency when they were looking at properties, having already been to see several that they'd found online which had turned out to be complete duds. The personal service from Bob and his small team; a receptionist and his junior partner, also known as his wife and daughter, had been second to none. He didn't publicise his properties on the large national websites, but instead, seemed to do a very good local trade and have a lot of people through his doors. Jim trusted him, and therefore he agreed to put the house on the market with him there and then.

By midday the next day, Mavis and Jim were viewing their third property of the morning; a three bedroom end of terrace property in a little village just a mile or so from Brooklands. The house was also only one mile from the school that Jim had most liked the look of, which meant it was in a perfect location. The estate agent informed Jim that there was no onward chain, and that whilst it was listed at three hundred and sixty thousand, he thought the owner might be willing to come down a little. Jim hadn't thought it would be possible to fall in love with a property at first glance, but the second he had walked through the door, he had felt completely at home. He was also encouraged by the fact that on the way into the small cul-de-sac, he had seen three families, all with children of around the same age as his boys, coming and going from their homes. That would mean there were other children around for the boys to make friends with. Just as they returned to the hallway, having toured the whole interior of the property and intending to go out into the garden next, Jim's mobile rang. He wouldn't normally have answered it whilst he was in a meeting of any description, but with so much going on in his life at the moment, and knowing that Peter was looking after the children, he felt it was probably best not to ignore the call.

Mavis followed the agent into the spacious and child friendly garden, as Jim lingered in the hallway. The call was Bob from the estate agency in Brighton.

"Hello Jim, great news. I think I have a buyer for your house, and the best part is, they're a cash buyer with no chain, so the sale could be quick too. They've made a preliminary offer of three hundred and thirty thousand, but I'll try to push them a bit higher for you". Jim was stunned. Once again, the stars seemed to be aligning and everything was working out for him. If he could get that amount for his home, then thanks to the nest egg Hannah's life insurance had provided, even if the vendors of this property wouldn't lower the price, he could probably just about afford it, although he'd need to factor in moving costs.

Thanking Bob for his call, he headed out to join the others in the garden, where Mavis was discussing with the estate agent where the children's play equipment could go and which flowerbeds would be best for growing home grown vegetables. Politely asking the agent if he could have a few moments alone with his mother-in-law, Jim asked Mavis what she thought of the property.

"Oh Jim, I think it's perfect. You and the boys could be so happy here" she gushed. Jim then explained what Bob had told him over the telephone.

"That's wonderful news Darling. Are you going to accept that offer and make one on this place?". Jim explained that his gut feeling was to tell the agent showing them around this house that he'd just received a cash offer for three hundred and thirty thousand pounds on his home, and that he would like to make an offer of the same value on this house. If Bob was able to persuade his prospective buyer to increase the offer for Jim's current house, then it would offer more bargaining power to Jim, but ultimately, he knew that he could pay the asking price for this property if needed.

Things moved very quickly after that. Jim's initial offer was rejected, but the vendor agreed to sell at three hundred and forty thousand pounds, and true to his word, Bob managed to push the potential buyer for Jim's house up to the same amount, meaning Jim would only be out of pocket by the moving costs. When they relayed all of this information to Peter upon returning to Dorking, his father-in-law was incredibly pleased and dared to voice something Mavis had been thinking all morning.

"That's our Hannah looking out for you son. She wants you to be happy and she's made all this happen for you". Jim was too emotional to respond, but deep down in his heart, he knew that Peter must have been right, because never had the process of securing a new job or buying and selling houses seemed easier.

25

Maddie and Adam spent every spare second of the weekend packing boxes. Helen had telephoned Maddie at Adam's office the previous day, to say that she had a client who was very interested in the property, and could she bring him round to view on the Saturday morning. The man in question was a young business tycoon, probably not yet thirty years old, who seemed to have more money than sense as far as Maddie was concerned, because he described the ten thousand dollars per month rental price as "very good value for such an awesome property" and literally signed on the dotted line that morning.

"I still don't get it" Maddie said, as she and Adam worked in the main bedroom, folding clothes into suitcases and packing the few trinkets he owned into boxes. "Why would you pay such an extortionate amount of money each month, just to rent somewhere?". Adam looked at her quizzically. Like Hank, the young man to whom this apartment would soon be home, Adam clearly didn't value money the way she did.

Maddie explained. "I pay nine hundred pounds per month in mortgage. Okay, so my house isn't anywhere near as big or swanky as this place, but it's home and more importantly, it's mine. I sort of understand paying silly money to buy somewhere like this, because clearly you made a terrific investment when you bought it, assuming that Helen is correct and it's actually doubled in value in the past three years, but surely if you've got the sort of money where you can afford to spend ten grand a month on your home, you'd want to buy somewhere?".

Adam paused for a moment then asked "is that a dig about me wanting to rent the flat in Canary Wharf?".

Maddie immediately regretted bringing up the conversation and was quick to reassure him "No, no, I get that because you only want somewhere for six months whilst you get the business off the ground and while we see whether we're going to make this work between us. That kind of makes sense, and you're only committing to six months and you're not paying out any more than I pay for my mortgage either. It's Hank, or anyone else for that matter, wanting to shell out the sort of money he's promised for this place that I don't get. I mean, for ten grand a month, surely he could buy somewhere decent and have an investment for his future?".

Adam thought for a moment then replied "We don't know his circumstances though do we Mads. Maybe, like me, he's only looking for short term. He's only signed up to rent for six months too".

Maddie knew this to be true, but still. "It just seems a lot of money to throw away in my opinion, but then I guess if he earns the sort of cash you do, maybe it doesn't seem like that big of a deal".

This was the crux of the problem Maddie realised. To her, ten thousand dollars, or pounds as she tended to think of it, was effectively three months gross salary. Working in his office over the past week, and seeing the incredible amount of money that Adam dealt with on a daily basis, not to mention now knowing how much money he earned, she recognised that to him, money didn't have quite the same value. Would she ever get used to the sort of extravagance that Adam took for granted? Adam had continually suggested that she should consider keeping her position as his personal assistant on a permanent basis too, as she had proven herself to be very effective in the role, not least by identifying Rosalie's misdemeanours, but also in liaising with clients and her meticulous attention to detail in paper based tasks. Maddie had promised to think about it, but she really didn't feel comfortable with the responsibility a post like that held, or with the idea of working for Adam indefinitely. She believed that if their relationship was going to work, and she really wanted it to, then she needed her own identity which was not connected to Adam, and had already vowed to speak to Fiona when she finally returned to the UK, because their visit to the Gingerbread exhibition in London between Christmas and New Year, combined with what she had learned this past week about business, had given her an idea that she wanted to share with her friend.

Hank, the person due to rent Adam's apartment, had been given the option of the penthouse being furnished or unfurnished when he took possession, and had opted for the former as apparently, he didn't own any furniture himself. This made the job of packing much easier, as they only had to worry about the personal effects Adam had accumulated, which were relatively few in number, and they didn't need to concern themselves with storing, selling or shipping the furniture. By mid-afternoon on Sunday, there were fifteen cardboard boxes and four suitcases stacked by the doors to the elevator. Maddie had arranged for a shipping company to collect them on the Thursday morning, and would therefore not be going into the office that day. All being well, Adam would finish up on the Thursday too, and they would both fly back to England on the Friday morning, landing that evening, although this very much depended on the transfer documentation being completed in time, the delays caused by Rosalie weighing heavily on both their minds. Hank was due to take possession of the property on 31st January, and Mrs Freeman, Adam's housekeeper, would deep clean the property in the interim, as well as checking in weekly to clean for Hank.

Satisfied that they could do no more in the apartment, Maddie suggested that they go for a walk. There was still snow on the ground, making it look and feel magical in the city, and she wanted to take the opportunity to experience as much of New York as she could before travelling home, because although she was confident that they would return to visit again at some point, she had no idea when. They decided that a walk along the picturesque Highline was in order. Until recently, Adam had never bothered with tourist attractions like this, but during her previous visit to New York, when they had first met, Maddie had encouraged him to explore the city more, and he and his parents had visited the Highline after Christmas.

"You know," Adam began, as they walked arm in arm along the old converted railroad "the last time I was here, I was talking about you".

Maddie looked up at the gorgeous man walking beside her, as she clutched his arm. "Oh really, good things I hope?" she joked.

"Well I came back to England, and I found you again, didn't I?" he replied.

Maddie pondered on thoughts of how much both their lives had transformed in just a few short weeks. On the Friday before Christmas, she had left home for work as usual, a job which she no longer held, as the company takeover had rendered her unemployed, and then had gone straight to the airport, flying out to the city which she loved most in the world; that same city which she once again found herself in now. By the Saturday lunchtime she had begun to believe that she'd made a terrible mistake, hating the idea of being alone for Christmas, and then Adam had unexpectedly walked into her life and since then they'd been on something of a whirlwind together. She had not believed that he would actually want to live in England again, and had known that she couldn't leave her family to live in New York herself, so she had ended their brief relationship on Boxing Day when she had returned to England alone. Thankfully, that was not to be the end of their story however, as he had, with the help of his parents, totally re-evaluated his life, and deciding that he wanted to make things work with her, he'd turned up on her door step. Now, less than a month after meeting, here they were packing up his life in New York and preparing to embark on new adventures together in England.

"Do you have any doubts?" Maddie asked him now, as they walked along admiring the view.

"Doubts about what?" Adam asked, unsure as to what she was intimating.

"Doubts about moving, about upping sticks and flying half way around the world to do something completely different?". Maddie knew that England would always be the place he considered home, but it was clear that he also very much enjoyed the lifestyle New York offered, and she couldn't help but wonder whether he really wanted to give it all up.

"No, absolutely none" came his very determined reply. Stopping them both in their tracks, he turned so that he was directly in front of Maddie and cupped her face tenderly in his hands.

"You are completely and utterly the best thing to happen to me in my whole life. Even if it wasn't for the new business, which I'm really excited about by the way, I would be happy returning to England because it would mean that I could be with you".

He kissed her gently, and for a few moments they were totally oblivious to their surroundings, until a couple of passing teenagers jeered at them, shouting "Oi!" and "Get a room!".

Breaking apart slightly, yet still with their arms wrapped around each other, Adam looked earnestly into Maddie's eyes as he said "I know that this has all moved very quickly between us, and I know that when we first met I said that I was determined to take this slowly, which I've been completely and utterly rubbish at, but I do know that we are meant to be together, and I don't for a second regret anything that has happened between us. Please tell me that you feel the same".

Surprised at his need for reassurance, as after all she was there in New York with him when her original plan for that Sunday afternoon had been a girls' afternoon out at the theatre in Wimbledon, she gazed lovingly into his eyes and said "I do, Adam, I definitely do feel the same" she kissed him gently on the lips then added "I love you, more than I ever thought it possible to love anyone, and I can't wait for the next chapter of our lives" and then, despite the potential of the teens returning, they were once more lost in a passionate embrace.

26

Jim had felt incredibly guilty requesting more time off when he'd handed in his notice, but he had arranged a meeting at the school that he wanted the boys to attend, and therefore missing a day's work was necessary. He drove up to Surrey as soon as he had dropped the children at school, and arrived in plenty of time for the meeting. The Headteacher, Mrs Brown, was a kindly lady to whom he immediately warmed to, and whilst he didn't really want to go through the whole tale of Hannah's accident again, as it made him hugely emotional whenever he relayed the story to anyone, he knew that it was important to give her all the details if his boys were going to become part of her school community.

Mrs Brown assured him that she would help the boys settle into the school, and that should it become necessary following the obvious trauma that they'd been through, not to mention the upheaval they were about to experience, she would organise suitable counselling for them. She then gave Jim a tour of the school, and he was certain that he spotted at least two of the children whom he'd seen with their families the previous Saturday when first viewing what was soon to be their new house, which only served to confirm in his mind that this was the right school for his children.

Completing all the necessary paperwork, and spending an absolute fortune on school uniforms, it was agreed that the boys would start their new school immediately after half term, although they would go for a taster session where they would both meet their new teachers and classmates on the Wednesday afternoon of the week before half term. Jim also signed the boys up for breakfast club, meaning that he could drop them off any time from 7.45am, and for the after school programme offered by the school which meant they would be entertained until 5pm each evening. Both of these activities had a cost attached to them, much like the similar programmes the boys went to currently, but this was still favourable to employing a childminder which would have been Jim's only other alternative.

Calling in to see Mavis and Peter on his way home, Jim updated them on all the latest developments concerning his move. He had signed all of the contracts with Claxton now, was looking forward to starting in March, and with the help of his new employer, Mark, he'd placed an order for his company car which he would collect on his first day.

"If I'm in the new house by then, I can drop the kids at school and then walk round to the office" he told his in laws, "but if things don't go to plan, then I might need to ask you guys for help on that day". They had agreed the previous weekend, despite Jim's reluctance to rely on the Baynes' for accommodation, that it would be best for Jim and the children to move out of their current house during the half term break, no matter what the state of play with the new house was. The solicitor and estate agents were working towards a completion date of Friday 21st February, which was in the half term holiday, but should there be any complications which caused delays, Jim and the children would relocate to Mavis and Peter's house on that Friday and stay there until they were able to move into their new home, so as to ensure that the children could be settled into their new school the following Monday.

"Obviously we would be more than happy to help" said Mavis, "but I don't think it's going to be a problem from what you've said. Hopefully you'll be in the new house by then".

Mavis and Peter had been so preoccupied with all the changes in Jim and their grandchildren's lives, that they had not thought much about Adam's impending relocation, but just as they were making plans with Jim, he telephoned them with an update.

"Hi Mum" he said, as Mavis picked up the telephone.

"Hello darling, how are you?" Mavis asked, surprised that he was calling when it was still so early in the morning in New York.

"I'm good thanks. In fact, I'm absolutely brilliant. I just wanted to let you know that I'll be back in England tomorrow night and I was kind of hoping that you or Dad might pick up me and Mads from Heathrow. Originally her sister was going to do it, but Juliet's double booked herself and so I said I'd ask you".

Mavis checked the calendar on her kitchen wall quickly, to make sure they had no other plans then said "Yes, that's no problem at all, and it will be lovely to see you both. How long will you be back for?". Adam laughed on the other end of the line.

"You still don't quite believe that I'm moving back home, do you mum?".

Mavis sighed. She really wanted to believe it, but until he was actually a permanent UK resident again, she wouldn't get her hopes up.

"I know you intend to darling, but I also know that you have a business to sell, a job to leave and a posh apartment to vacate, and all that takes time so I'm under no illusions that you're going to be back here permanently for quite some time yet".

Adam immediately felt guilty for not keeping his family better informed of events in New York. The lack of communication with his family, that he had previously been so guilty of, was exactly what he had promised himself would change, and Maddie had even nagged him to call his parents the previous weekend when he told her that he'd not spoken to them since returning to America, but he simply hadn't got round to it. Vowing once again that he would endeavour to speak to his parents more regularly in future, he shared the good news with his mother that he had already sold the majority of his shares in the business, releasing enough equity to invest in the planned venture with Ed, so Stephen would be taking over from him as CEO at Spruce with effect that afternoon, once the transfer of share ownership paperwork was officially signed, sealed and delivered which was due to happen at a Board meeting at 10am that morning. He then added that, thanks to Maddie, a tenant had been found for his apartment and all his belongings were being shipped back to the UK that very morning.

"Bottom line is, when we come home tomorrow, aside from the odd fleeting business trip which will likely bring me back here, I'll be home for good".

When Mavis returned to the lounge, having taken the call from Adam in the kitchen, she was sobbing.

"Sweetheart, whatever's wrong?" asked Peter as she walked back into the room, immediately concerned that the phone had brought bad news.

"I'm not upset darling" she said, through her tears, "I'm happy, oh so happy. Adam's coming home tomorrow. All of my family will be back living close to me again. Forever." Mavis went on to explain to Jim and Peter all that Adam had told her.

"Wow, he really did move quickly, didn't he" Peter commented.

"I think it's Hannah" said Mavis. "I think she's guiding my boys back home and I think she's the one that's made it so easy for Jim and Adam to relocate".

Jim wasn't sure how to react to that. He couldn't argue that things were moving remarkably quickly and easily for two people moving house, and that they had been incredibly lucky with the simplicity of each relocation, but much as he wanted to believe it was his wife looking down on them all, he had never been one to believe in angels and preferred not to think of Hannah in that way.

The following evening, when Maddie and Adam disembarked the plane at Heathrow, Adam had an overwhelming feeling of being at home. He didn't actually know where he would be spending that night, as he was torn between wanting to go to Maddie's house with her, and a sense of loyalty to his parents meaning that he really should spend the night in their house with them, particularly as they were playing chauffeur that evening, but what he did know, was that he was back where he belonged. He would worry about the other details as time progressed, as they were of minor consequence compared to being home.

Mavis was overjoyed when Maddie and Adam walked through the arrivals gate to greet them. She enveloped first her son, and then his girlfriend, in huge hugs and then stood aside so that her husband could do the same.

"Welcome home both of you" she said, enthusiastically, "it's so good to have you back".

"It's good to be back too, mum" Adam replied.

When they reached Maddie's home, she invited them in for a drink, although soon realised that she didn't have any milk to offer them in tea or coffee. Peter offered to pop down to the local shop for her, and Adam went too, leaving Mavis and Maddie alone for a few moments.

"You have no idea how grateful I am to you Maddie" Mavis said, for what must be at least the third time during their brief acquaintance. "Thanks to you, my biggest boy is home for good, and I am absolutely over the moon". She then went on to tell Maddie about Jim's move. Maddie knew the village where he was planning on moving to, as it was very close to where her friend Fiona lived, and said that she would be more than willing to help out with childcare until she managed to find herself a permanent job. Mavis promised to pass that offer on to Jim, although she was secretly hopeful that Maddie would soon see Jim for herself and be able to make the offer in person.

27

"Happy Birthday to you, Happy Birthday to you, Happy Birthday dear Milly, Happy Birthday to you!!" the whole of Maddie's extended family had gathered at Josh's house to celebrate the fifth birthday of her niece Amelia. As she blew out the candles on the unicorn cake which her mother Jen had lovingly made for her, Milly smiled the goofiest of smiles and revelled in the cheers of "Hip-Hip Hooray" that followed.

Scooping her niece up into her arms, Maddie said "I can't believe that you're five now Mills! That means you're a big grown up girl doesn't it?"

Looking at her aunt with the utmost seriousness, Milly replied "yes, but I'm still your favourite littlest girl aren't I Auntie Mads".

Maddie laughed "of course you are, and Alice is my favourite biggest girl and Tilly and Lucy are my favourite middle-sized ones" referring to her three other nieces.

Amelia's actual birthday had been the day before, the Saturday, and despite her jetlag, Maddie had kept her promise and been there for her birthday party with her friends from school. Josh had booked a party at the local soft play centre, which had been noisy and chaotic, but at least the staff there had done the majority of the work. Maddie and her sister Juliet had been there to help out, but they found themselves relatively redundant as there was very little to do. They had therefore spent most of the afternoon catching up with Josh and Jenny, the other adults present, whilst the children ran around like lunatics, wearing themselves out.

Today was Milly's 'family' party, and all of Maddie's siblings had come, together with their partners and children, and Jenny's parents and sister and her family were also in attendance, having travelled down from the Midlands to celebrate with the birthday girl. Maddie found herself in high demand from all her various nieces and nephews who all adored her, and who had missed her terribly during her time in New York, as they usually saw her every weekend and often in the week too. Between playing cards with Ethan and Alice, helping Oliver and Timmy build a Lego space station and dressing up Barbie dolls with Lucy, Matilda and Amelia, Maddie hardly spoke to Adam or any of the other adults for the whole time that they were there.

"You really do love kids, don't you" said Adam as they finally left Josh's house, late on the Sunday night, Maddie having been required to stay for bedtime so that she could read the birthday girl a story.

"Yes, they're my world" replied Maddie, referring to the children in her family.

"Not just those guys though. You were so good with my nephews too" Adam recalled, remembering just how quickly Maddie had apparently won Jamie around when she'd first met him.

"I've always loved kids, and although I've never been lucky enough to have children myself, I've made sure that I'm the best auntie I can be, and I think kids see that in me" then turning the tables on him she asked "did you ever want kids?".

Adam wasn't really sure. He liked the idea of having children, and always imagined that he would one day have them, yet it had never been something he'd seriously considered, until now.

"I guess I've never really been in a position to consider having kids" he said, "so I'd not really thought about it until you asked, but I think I'd like to be a dad one day". Now it was Maddie's turn to be slow in responding. She would love to have children, but she also knew that her body clock had been ticking away for years and the chances of her being able to conceive now were far less than had she met Adam ten years previously. There was no way that they were ready for children in their relationship yet, as it was still so early on, but he'd just told her that he would like to be a dad one day and she felt that she ought to at least highlight the fact that biologically, they might not find it easy to become parents if that was something they decided upon later down the line.

"I'd love children too" she began, "but if I'm honest, one of the reasons I've made such an effort with my nieces and nephews is so that I can be a sort of surrogate mum to them. At my age, it wouldn't be easy to have children now". Adam pointed out that they'd just discovered that Francesca and Ed, who were similar ages to them, were about to become parents again, and to twins, so nothing was impossible. Maddie agreed that this was true, however she was quick to point out that the two of them still had a lot of other hurdles to overcome before thinking about babies, like making sure that they were both gainfully employed.

Throughout the following week, Maddie and Adam spent most of their time together, meeting up with Ed whenever possible, to get things moving on the new business. Ed had resigned from his current post, and would be free to plough his energy full time into the new business from 2nd March, but in the meantime, he was taking as many days off as his leave allowance would permit, and when working from home could spare a few hours here and there to liaise with Adam.

By the Friday evening, Maddie reported to Juliet and Fiona as they met for dinner at a local Pizzeria, that they had now secured premises for the new business. In addition, Adam had taken possession of the flat he was renting and moved his belongings, which had arrived from the US, into it. Also, with a little bit of help from her brother Paul, who happened to be a website designer, Smithers, Baynes and Co now had a brand spanking new website and company logo.

"I'm so jealous of you Mads" Juliet said, as they sipped her glass of mineral water, cursing herself for agreeing to do 'dry January' meaning that she couldn't share the bottle of wine Maddie and Fiona had ordered, although in fairness it was also her turn to be the designated driver, so she wouldn't have been drinking anyway.

"How so?" asked Maddie, surprised at the vehemence her sister had thrown into that comment.

"Well, for starters, you've got this amazing new bloke who is stonking rich, and you're still in that wonderful honeymoon phase of your romance where everything in life is fabulous, but more than that, you've got this exciting new business venture going on which means you have a real purpose in life. All I've got is part time work as a shop assistant in Boots, a grumpy husband who really needs to drink some alcohol soon before I kill him, and two completely crazy children".

Maddie and Fiona both laughed at their friend. "It's not funny!" she argued.

"Oh but Jules, it really is" said Fiona. "We all know that you and Tom are crazy about each other, and that you wouldn't change him for the world, or the kids come to that, but when you told us on New Year's Eve that you were planning on giving up alcohol for January we all knew that this would happen!".

Juliet tried to look offended, but she failed miserably. "See, that's what I mean" she pouted, "I'm boring and predictable".

"What if I said that I have a plan which could change all three of our lives?" Maddie asked, not wanting to dwell on her sister's melancholy mood longer than necessary.

"Sounds interesting" replied Fiona, "do tell!". Maddie finally then got the opportunity to moot the idea that she had been considering since she was in New York.

"I don't want to work for Adam indefinitely, and I obviously need to have something to pay the bills and to keep myself busy, because rich as Adam might be, I've always been independent, and I don't want that to change now. Working for Houlton, I recognised where I went wrong with my catering firm. That folded purely and simply because I was too nice, and I allowed bad payers to bring me down, but during my time at Houlton, and most especially in the past few weeks working alongside Adam, I've learned a lot about business and I'd like to use Dad's money to try again".

Juliet and Fiona both looked expectantly at Maddie. She said that her idea could change all of their lives, but so far, she hadn't given them any indication as to how. "I would like to open a bakery" said Maddie, "and I'd like you two to come in with me as partners". Initially, when the idea had first come to Maddie, she'd envisaged it just being herself and Fiona in the partnership, as they were the two with catering expertise, but in recognising the importance of capital for start-up businesses, realising that her own inheritance alone wouldn't cover it, and knowing that Juliet actually had a lot of experience and expertise in retail, she'd decided to include her sister in the grand plan she'd been plotting.

"My vision is that Fiona, you would be the lead baker, as you are by far the best pastry chef and cake maker that I have ever met, and that Jules you would be in charge of the retail aspect of the business, and that I would have a duel role, managing the books and running the business side of things, whilst also supporting Fi with the actual baking. If I've learned anything from working with Adam recently, it's that there's a lot of money required for a start-up, and we wouldn't earn a huge amount in the early days, but I honestly think we'd have a lot of fun doing this together, and I also think that we have the potential to make it a huge success. What do you say ladies?"

Both Fiona and Juliet were stunned, and neither knew quite what to say at first, although the more Maddie talked through her ideas, the more enthusiastic they both became. Promising that they would go home and discuss it with their husbands, both ladies acknowledged that they would relish the challenge of doing something like this, and that they were both ready for something new in their lives.

28

"You'll never guess what news I've had this weekend" Francesca said to Sandi, as they had their usual breakfast gossip session. Francesca and Ed had been to Fiona and Jeremy's house for Sunday lunch the previous day, and having obtained Jeremy's blessing for Maddie's business idea, Fiona had outlined the plans for their new bakery venture to her family.

"Please don't tell me there are more babies involved, because I really don't think I could cope if you announced you were actually carrying triplets" joked Sandi.

Francesca laughed, "no, nothing like that. In fact, it's not really my news to tell, it's Fi's. She's going into business with her old university friend Maddie and Maddie's sister Juliet" Francesca explained.

"Isn't Maddie the one that's dating the guy that's starting a new business with Ed?" Sandi asked.

"Yes, that's right" she confirmed.

"Blimey, you need to watch out Ches. This starting a business thing is clearly contagious in your family". Both of them dissolved into hysterical laughter at that comment. Francesca quipped back that it was an ailment requiring a doctor better than she to cure, before giving Sandi the details as she knew them.

"The business is going to be a bakery come coffee shop, probably somewhere that's equidistant between their three homes, and there are loads of empty units around at the moment, so they're going to look at a few and enquire about taking one on" explained Francesca.

"Wow, that's a big step, but good on her if she can make it work" Sandi replied. "We all know what an amazing chef Fiona is, and from what you've said Maddie used to run a catering firm too didn't she, so I guess a bakery makes sense, but it's a lot to take on with the family and everything".

Francesca nodded. "Jez thinks Fi's bored with being a housewife now that the kids don't need her so much, and he's totally behind her on this. AJ's away at Uni most of the time now, and the boys are typical teenagers who rely on her more as a taxi service and a source of funding for their social lives, than anything else and even little Sal's growing so rapidly that she doesn't really need Fi to be at home all day anymore, plus Dad will help out if she's stuck for childcare, just like he supports me. If I'm honest, I'm amazed that Fi's stayed at home as long as she has. I'd have been fed up years ago, but she was always so determined to be a stay at home Mum. I admire her" Francesca said earnestly.

"Well my news from the weekend is nowhere near as exciting" Sandi countered, desperate to fill Francesca in on the news of yet another disastrous date, "but it will sure make you laugh". She went on to explain that she'd been on a date with a guy she'd met on Tinder. Firstly, he looked nothing like his profile picture and had far more acne than any teenager she'd ever met, and secondly, all he could talk about for the entire date was his total obsession with collecting car registration numbers. Worst of all, Sandi literally couldn't get a word in edge ways for the first two hours they were there.

"Now that I do find hard to believe" Francesca said with a chuckle, knowing that most people would say that of Sandi and not the other way around.

"No, honestly Ches, it was awful. Every time I opened my mouth to try and make my excuses to leave, he started again, and he had the most droning of voices. In the end I got up and went to the loo, him still mid conversation, and I looked up the telephone number for the pub on the internet and called them and explained that I was on a really bad date and trapped hiding from him in the ladies. The barmaid took me seriously, thank goodness, and came in to find me. I relayed everything to her, and she said she'd get her colleague to distract him whilst she snuck me out of the pub!".

By this point, Francesca was literally roaring with laughter. "I can't believe it was that bad" she half stated, half questioned.

"Oh Ches, it was worse than bad. I've deleted my Tinder profile and I'm seriously considering changing the number plate on my car in case he tries to track me through it. I was looking online last night but it costs hundreds. He said when he arrived that he'd made a note of all the number plates in the car park. I'm telling you Ches, he was a proper freak!". Both of them were still laughing so much that tears were streaming down their faces when the first of the other GPs, Dr David Ghaffar, arrived for morning surgery.

"What's so funny?" asked the young male GP who had won the hearts of lots of their female clientele for his stunning looks.

"Ask Sand about her date" said Francesca, standing and gathering her belongings. "I've got to prepare for morning surgery, but she'll fill you in".

Francesca didn't think she had laughed so much in weeks, months even, as she had that morning. She considered herself very lucky that she had such a wonderful husband in Ed, even if he was very preoccupied at the moment. She had to admit she was getting a little tired of listening to financial predictions for the business, and endless names of potential clients he intended to approach once they were up and running, which he randomly kept bringing up in conversation, but no one could ever describe her dynamic, career driven husband as boring. It was simply that she wasn't interested in business. Even though there was a business role to play as part of her job, she left the majority of the organisational decisions to Sandi, because to her it was the patients that were most important. She loved being able to look at the symptoms which were presented to her by her patients and investigate what the cause might be before establishing the right treatments. It was like being a detective, except that the crimes were illnesses.

Ed telephoned Francesca at lunchtime to inform her that he'd just sold the last of the shares necessary to provide his share of the capital for Smithers, Baynes and Co. This meant that the business could finally get underway. Francesca loved that he'd called her at work, even though that particular piece of information could easily have waited until they were at home together that evening. It meant that he wanted her to be fully involved, even though she didn't understand the majority of what the business required of him. They were a team, and they shared things. Oh, how she wished Sandi could find someone like Ed to be a team with.

Ed was over the moon. He had done it. He had raised every penny he'd promised Adam, and not only that, but due to some very clever investments over the years, he'd managed to hang onto enough shares elsewhere to maintain a reasonable income for his family whilst he and Adam got things underway, as they'd both agreed not to draw a salary from the business for the first six months.

In Ed's mind, 2020 was going to be his year. For so many years now, his life had been about other people. In the early days working in the city, it was all about making money for other people, whilst trying to carve out a reputation for himself. Once he'd finally started to become successful in his own right, he'd asked Francesca to marry him, and he'd anticipated them living a luxurious life together, with him focused on his career and her on hers, for the first few years at least. That had all been thrown over when Sally and Tim had been killed, and suddenly Ed's priorities changed, and his life was put on hold. Literally overnight, he went from being something of a city playboy to playing stepdad to two gorgeous little girls, and like their official guardian, his fiancé Francesca, they melted his heart in a way that he had never imagined possible. From the moment that he moved in with Francesca and the girls, Ed's life changed beyond all recognition, but he didn't regret a single second. When he and Francesca finally married, and the girls began referring to him as Dad, he felt like he had achieved far more than anything he had ever set out to do. When the boys had come along later, he'd loved being a footie dad with Doug, and playing in the park or building endless Lego models with Danny. Now, whilst he was truly excited about becoming a father to twins, he knew that he needed more. He'd coasted at work for so long, making money but not really having a purpose. Now he could build a business which would be his legacy to all six of his children and he could really create a name for himself in the business world as his surname, Smithers, would be in the company title.

Looking over the figures that he and Adam had been working on earlier that morning, Ed wished that he could get started on contacting potential clients straight away, but he knew he was bound to his current company for the next four weeks, and it would be considered bad practice to make contact when he was on their time. He had waited this long for this opportunity to present itself. He could wait another few weeks. 2020 was going to be his best year ever.

29

Once Maddie, Fiona and Juliet had decided their venture was a go, much like Adam and Ed, there was no stopping them. They quickly secured a suitable shop premises and began the process of getting it fitted out with the latest state of the art baking equipment.

"This kitchen's starting to look like Adam's penthouse in New York" Maddie commented, as she and Fiona admired all of the smart stainless-steel equipment being installed.

"It looks like something out of a spaceship to me" replied Fiona "are you sure we'll work out how to use it all?" she joked.

"We'll be fine. Trust me" said Maddie.

Fiona did trust Maddie, and so did Juliet. Each of them had agreed to contribute the same amount of funding into the venture, to ensure that they were equal partners, and they'd opted for the name 'Sweet and Delicious' for the shop. Juliet was in charge of designing and organising the shop floor, whilst Maddie and Fiona had taken on the task of organising the kitchen and acquiring the necessary baking equipment. Maddie and Juliet's brother Paul had once again been drafted in to create a website and logo for the bakery, and the girls had been incredibly impressed with the results.

"I've had these flyers printed up" said Juliet, joining the others in the kitchen of the new premises where tradesmen were working tirelessly on their behalf, and I've ordered ten little silver bistro tables and some matching chairs for the shop floor. I've kept it small to start with, but if we find they're all being utilised, then we can get some more, and maybe even get some to go under the awning outside, but I don't want to crowd the space unnecessarily". All being well, they would be opening the store on the 2nd March, which was only a few weeks away now, so they really were making rapid progress.

"Hello, anyone here?" they heard Jeremy's voice from the main shop door.

"Hang on a minute Jez, we're just coming out" Fiona called back.

"Wow, you're making real headway here ladies" Jeremy said, genuinely impressed with the pink, white and silver colour scheme that greeted him and the sleek display cabinets just crying out to be filled with his wife's baking. "The place looks absolutely fantastic, although it's little wonder the amount I've seen, or rather not seen, my wife in the past couple of weeks". Fiona looked a little crestfallen. She was really excited by Sweet and Delicious, but the last thing she wanted was for it to interfere with her marriage or family.

"I'm joking Fi" he corrected himself quickly, realising that he'd said the wrong thing. "I think what you've done is amazing, but I did wonder whether you might have time for lunch, being as I've got the day off today". Relaxing a little and relishing the possibility of a rare opportunity for lunch alone with her husband, Fiona agreed immediately and said her goodbyes to the others.

"How's about you and me have lunch together too babe?" said Juliet, her stomach suddenly realising that she'd not eaten all day and complaining loudly about it at the mention of food.

"Sure, I'd love that" said Maddie. Although they'd spent lots of time together working recently, it had been a while since Maddie had socialised with her sister and like Fiona, she relished the chance for them to spend some quality time together.

"So, how's things with you and Adam?" Juliet asked, as they sat down for lunch in Nando's nearby.

"Good, I think" replied Maddie.

"If you don't mind me saying Mads, and you know I'll always be brutally honest with you, you really don't sound too sure about that. Please don't tell me that the honeymoon is over already. Not after everything that the two of you have been through". Maddie shook her head. It wasn't that they didn't have the same degree of passion when they saw each other, it was just that since they returned from America, she'd hardly seen him. Also, their conversation about babies was playing on her mind. Explaining all of this to Juliet she asked "what if he decides a year or two down the line that he wants kids and it's too late for me Jules? What do we do then?".

Exhaling with a whistle through her teeth, Juliet replied "I think you just have to be honest and upfront with him now, which it sounds like you were, and then cross that bridge if and when you come to it Mads. There's no use worrying about something you're powerless to change. What you can do though, is make more time for Adam now. I reckon if you saw more of each other, then you'd feel much more secure about your relationship".

Maddie knew that Juliet was right, but it wasn't that easy. Adam had spent most of the past few weeks at his flat in Canary Wharf, because it was close to the premises that he and Ed were converting for their business and he wanted to oversee the building work, and when he wasn't there, he and his parents were down in Brighton helping his brother-in-law pack in preparation for moving house the following week. Similarly, she'd spent most of her time at her own house because of its proximity to the new bakery, so in the time since they had returned from America, they'd only spent five nights under the same roof. Even at the weekends, they hadn't seen much of each other, as they'd both been focused on their own families and on their respective business ventures, and she didn't anticipate them spending much quality time together this coming weekend either, because she had promised to look after Ethan, Matilda and Oliver from Saturday lunchtime to Sunday lunchtime to enable Paul and Mandy to go away overnight for their wedding anniversary, which was as much a thank you to Paul for all his work on the various websites as anything else.

"If it would help, I could have Paul's kids?" Juliet offered.

"No, honestly, it's fine. Adam will probably spend most of the weekend in Brighton anyway. Thank you for offering though" Maddie replied, grateful to have finally unloaded how she was feeling to someone.

"Look Mads" said her sister, in her most determined tone. "It's Friday, we're not going to get much done this afternoon with the builders in the way, so why don't we all take the rest of today off. Fi can spend some proper quality time with Jeremy, you can go and see Adam, wherever in the country he is, because remember he is now in the same country as you which is a definite improvement on the position when we last discussed your relationship like this, and then next week we can regroup" adding, almost as an afterthought "although I should warn you, I'm going to be about as useful as a chocolate tea pot next week when the kids are on half term".

This made Maddie giggle. She knew exactly what Juliet meant, as her children were known to leave destruction and devastation in their wake, meaning anything Juliet did the following week would probably require a clear up operation after her kids, but she also loved them dearly, and knew that chances were that she would end up looking after them as much as her sister, rendering her less effective too.

"Okay, you text Fi and tell her not to rush back and I'll locate Adam. You're right. At least he's not going to be more than a hundred miles away now. It's a huge improvement on having the Atlantic Ocean between us".

Adam was surprised to see Maddie's number on his caller display when she telephoned, as they'd both been so engrossed in work that they had barely made contact all week, but as he saw her name pop up on the screen his heart skipped a beat and he suddenly felt so much happier.

"Hey Mads, how are you doing?" he asked.

"I'm good actually" she replied. "My sister has convinced me that I need an afternoon and evening off, so I was wondering if I could meet you somewhere? I've missed you" she added.

"I would absolutely love that" he replied earnestly. "It feels like I've barely spoken to you, let alone seen you this week. I've missed you too".

All of a sudden, the unease she had been feeling evaporated and she felt much happier. "Great, where should we meet? Your place or mine?".

Agreeing that Adam would come to her house, because he had something that he wanted to show her, they arranged to meet in two hours' time. She dashed home, and quickly prepared a pasta dish for their dinner, then jumped in the shower, feeling grimy having been around all the shop fitting work earlier. She'd just finished pampering herself, when he arrived. She opened the door to find him hidden behind a beautiful large bouquet of lilies, which she took from him.

As she tried to usher him in from the cold, he said "actually, would you put your coat on and come out for a minute instead?" Doing as he asked, she followed him outside and saw a brand new Audi TT parked on her driveway.

"What do you think?" he asked. The car was truly beautiful with leather interior and shiny silver paintwork.

"It's lovely" she said, "but what happened to the hire car". Adam looked sheepish.

"I kind of pranged it when I was reversing out of Jim's drive the other day, and although it was only a tiny dent, and not entirely my fault as the rose bush obscured my view of the gatepost that I hit, I decided it was better to own a car than to keep renting one. After all, a wise person once told me that if you had the money to do so, it was more cost effective in the long term to buy than to rent". Maddie laughed. She knew he was referring to the conversation they'd had about Hank when packing up his apartment in New York.

"That's very true, but if you prang a car, that's not very cost effective either" she said teasingly.

"That's also correct, but this one has reversing sensors, so I'm sure I'll be okay" he retorted, and with that they made their way inside for a cosy evening together working on their most important mutual venture; their relationship.

30

The end of February and the beginning of March brought new beginnings for everyone. Jim and the boys were able to move into their new home on the Friday at the end of the school half term break, ably assisted by Adam, Maddie, Mavis and Peter, who all spent the weekend together, helping Jim and the boys unpack and turn their new house into a home. The boys' bedrooms were lovingly painted by Maddie, who unveiled painting and decorating as another skill that she possessed, and she even managed to add some hand painted designs on the walls to personalise them. Jamie's room had the best impression Maddie could manage of Brighton Pier emblazoned on the wall, as a reminder of somewhere he considered to be a favourite place, whilst for Robbie she had painted Mickey and Minnie Mouse, characters whom he was ever so slightly obsessed with now that he knew he was going to visit Disneyworld later in the year. All the family had been incredibly impressed by her efforts, and the boys threw their arms around her in thanks upon seeing their newly decorated rooms.

By the time they started at their new school on the Monday morning, the boys had met and made friends with the two boys living next door who were of similar ages. Sam was, it transpired, a huge fan of football and within minutes of meeting Jamie, he had invited him round to shoot goals in his back garden. Jim had been slightly nervous about letting Jamie go, but Mavis had encouraged him that it was a good thing that Jamie wanted to play, and the neighbours all seemed very welcoming and friendly. Robbie had established that Toby, the younger boy living next door, was also a Peppa Pig, Mickey Mouse and Paw Patrol fan, so Robbie asked his father whether Toby could "come round to my house to play".

Encouraged by the use of the term 'my house' so soon, Jim had agreed and so the beginnings of a new friendship were forged. The two families even walked to school together the next morning, and Elaine, the boys' mother, explained to Jim that there were three other families living in the road with children at the same school and they often helped each other out with childcare, so to ask if he needed anything. It would be a while before Jim felt confident to ask anyone other than his family for help, but it was reassuring to know that the offer was there.

For Adam and Ed, their business officially went live on 2nd March, the same day as Maddie, Fiona and Juliet's bakery. Ed went home to Francesca that evening raving about the wonderfully successful day they'd had, and the number of clients who had not only agreed to follow him from his previous job, but who had "put their money where their mouths are" and actually taken business to them on the first day.

"I don't think I've seen you this excited about a day at work for years" commented Francesca as they lay next to each other in bed that evening.

"You don't mind, do you?" he asked, conscious that she was struggling through her final few weeks at work, and finding it incredibly difficult to keep going.

"No darling, of course not. I love that you're so happy" she said, leaning across as best she could to kiss him. Francesca was suddenly huge. Her pregnancy might have gone undetected in the first four months, but there was no mistaking it now and she could definitely feel the twins fighting each other for room inside of her. The next eleven weeks until her delivery date couldn't pass soon enough as far as she was concerned.

Fiona, Juliet and Maddie had an equally successful opening day. The leafleting which Juliet had done in half term with her children, along with a few of her other nieces and nephews and Fiona's daughter Sally, had proved to be an extremely successful tactic. Not only had it kept the children out of the way whilst Fiona and Maddie got the kitchen running and acquired all the necessary certifications for food hygiene and the like, but it also meant that they did a roaring trade on their opening day, despite it being a wet and miserable March Monday. Via the website they took orders for five of Fiona's famed birthday cakes, which she had been making for friends and family for years so there were lots of photos to showcase, and the footfall through the door was better than they ever could have expected. Best of all, many of those who visited on the Monday kept returning throughout the rest week and beyond.

At the surgery, Sandi had solved the problem of a replacement for Francesca's maternity leave, managing to secure a fully qualified ex-army medic called Samantha who was willing to start immediately, meaning that Francesca could hand over gradually and not worry so much about the practice. Samantha had left the army when her children were born and had qualified as a GP through Parkside surgery once they started school, but with her husband still being an army officer, she had been stationed abroad for the past ten years. Upon their return to the UK for him to take up a new posting at a local barracks, Samantha had popped into Parkside to see whether there were still any familiar faces working there. Sandi and Francesca had been thrilled to see her again and had asked her whether she might consider taking the job. As her husband's current posting was going to be for two years, the timing was perfect, and Francesca was able to leave knowing that her patients would be in good hands.

Jim started working for Claxton and loved every second of his new job. It was a very different type of challenge to what he'd been used to, but he really enjoyed meeting all the Practice Managers and GPs and enjoyed getting to know hospital personnel too. Finally, he had a job which was rewarding, rather than mundane, and part of him wished that he'd been brave enough to look for other jobs when Sphere had relocated, rather than moving his family to Brighton, but he didn't dwell on the past as he couldn't change it, and just concentrated on building a future for his family. He became a regular visitor at Parkside and found himself striking up quite a friendship with Sandi, who always greeted him with the same friendly question; "a cuppa and a biscuit Jim?" and made him laugh out loud at her hilarious antics.

As everyone came together at the bakery on the last Sunday in March to celebrate Maddie's birthday, she couldn't quite believe how her own fairytale, and that of the others there to celebrate with her, had come true. She and Adam had settled into a routine of spending one night at his place in Canary Wharf, and then the next in her house in Walton. They both spent Saturday mornings working, but once the bakery closed at lunchtime, Adam also logged off from work and it was all about their families.

Adam had one more surprise lined up though. The same group of people who had gathered together at Maddie's house on New Years' Eve, and who had witnessed Adam's heartfelt plea to Maddie to give him a second chance to prove his love for her, plus Mavis, Peter, Jim and the boys who had joined in the birthday celebrations, found themselves witnessing a proposal of marriage. Just after Maddie had cut the absolutely stunning cake made by Fiona for the occasion, Adam had asked if he could have everyone's attention. Having silenced the room, even the children, he got down on one knee and produced a simple, but absolutely beautiful diamond ring.

"Madeline Lane. You are the love of my life and I know now that I never, ever want to be parted from you again. Please would you do me the honour of agreeing to become my wife".

As Maddie said "yes" and he placed the ring on her finger, the crowded room erupted with cheers of congratulations.

Watching her son and his new fiancé, Mavis turned to Peter and quietly whispered, so that only he would hear. "This is Hannah. She's made this happen".

Peter hugged his wife close and said "yes, my dear, I believe you're right".

Adam stood and Maddie fell into his arms. They had started the year with a similar embrace, and a similar public display of their emotions, but on that particular evening, they had not really known where time would take them. Now, three full months down the line, they were sure. They were meant to be together and they would spend the rest of their lives finding their happy ever after, just like in all the fairytales. This was their fairytale reality.

ABOUT THE AUTHOR

Helen Claringbull is a Music Teacher in a Secondary School in the South East of England. Having always had a passion for reading and writing, she finally put pen to paper in 2006, yet it was several years later that her first novel, The Greatest Gift, was finally published.

A Fairytale Reality is Helen's third novel, and in this book, she has continued the story started in her first 'Fairytale' book, A Fairytale Christmas. In exploring the future that Maddie and Adam carve out for themselves, Helen has found the perfect opportunity to entwine their lives with those characters we first met in The Greatest Gift, meaning that this book is a sequel in every sense of the word, and one which Helen has truly enjoyed writing.

Helen hopes that this book will be just as well received as her first two novels, and looks forward to continuing the Fairytale series in 2020, as she doesn't yet believe that these characters have had their final happy ending.

Printed in Great Britain
by Amazon